Josie's heart slammed against her chest as adrenalin ricocheted through her body. She could barely make out the features of the enormous man standing at the foot of the bed, but she'd swear she could feel his anger.

'What do you want?' It was a reflex question—one she wasn't sure she wanted to hear the answer to—and it came out as a shaky whisper.

'I *want* my bed.'

'What do you mean, *your* bed? Who the hell are *you*?'

'Connor Preston. I own this place,' he said. 'Who are *you*?'

The gruff timbre of the voice coming at her through the gloom was unnerving.

'I'm Abigail's business partner—Josie Marchpane. Abi said I could stay here for a while...' She tailed off as his expression grew darker.

'Is that right?' He was abrupt now, unfriendly.

'Look, do you mind?' She forced her shoulders back and tipped up her chin. 'I'm not exactly prepared for socialising right now. Can we talk about this in the morning?'

Connor dragged his gaze up from where her fingers grasped the towel and frowned. 'Where am I supposed to sleep? You've taken the only bed.'

'If I'd known you were coming we could have worked something out.'

'Worked something out, huh?'

He dropped his gaze down her body, taking in the swell of her figure that the towel barely concealed. The disturbing throb began again, deep inside her. She reached round and pulled the towel tighter, unnerved by his attention. It was disconcerting, being half-naked in front of a total stranger. Especially one as unsettling as Connor Preston.

Dear Reader

Ah, the South of France—home of the *most* delicious sun-ripened tomatoes, Mediterranean storms and the sultry air of pleasure and possibility. The ideal setting for a workaholic with a chip on her shoulder to lose her inhibitions and finally start to *live*.

As characters on a page Connor and Josie have been on a long journey together. They've been shacked up in the electronic ether for a few years now, but they just wouldn't let me into their secret world until I picked them up again a year or so ago and they finally started talking to me. Suddenly I *got* them—and about time too!

I love these two together. They're both headstrong and determined but with a soft centre, both crying out for kindness and patience and a deeper understanding of what they intrinsically need. They've been running from their pasts and the weight of expectations for so long they've lost their way. Until they're forced to share a house, sit still for once and *talk*.

I hope you enjoy travelling with them on their journey to emotional freedom and love as much as I did.

With best wishes

Christy X

HOLIDAY WITH
A STRANGER

BY
CHRISTY McKELLEN

Published in Great Britain 2014
by Mills & Boon, an imprint of Harlequin (UK) Limited,
Eton House, 18-24 Paradise Road, Richmond, Surrey, TW9 1SR

© 2014 Christy McKellen

ISBN: 978 0 263 24187 7

Harlequin (UK) Limited's policy is to use papers that are natural,
renewable and recyclable products and made from wood grown in
sustainable forests. The logging and manufacturing processes conform
to the legal environmental regulations of the country of origin.

Printed and bound in Great Britain
by CPI Antony Rowe, Chippenham, Wiltshire

B000 000 011 3986

BK (Before Kids) **Christy McKellen** worked as a video and radio producer in London and Nottingham. After a decade of dealing with nappies, tantrums and endless questions from toddlers she has come out the other side and moved into the wonderful world of literature. She now spends her time writing flirty, sexy romance with a kick—her dream job!

In her downtime she can be found drinking the odd glass of champagne, ambling around the beautiful South West of England, or escaping from real life by dashing off to foreign lands with her fabulous family.

Christy loves to hear from readers. You can contact her at:

www.christymckellen.blogspot.com
http://www.facebook.com/christymckellenauthor
https://twitter.com/ChristyMcKellen

**This is Christy McKellen's debut for Modern Tempted™
and is available in eBook format
from www.millsandboon.co.uk**

Where do I start with the thanks? So many people have supported and encouraged me with my writing through the years. First of all my wonderful family. What would I do without you? You believed I could do it even when I didn't.

To my brilliant critique partners: Jill Steeples, Cait O'Sullivan and Lucy Oliver. Thank you for the generous loan of your eagle eyes and the time you took to read the manuscript and help me make it sparkle.

To Aimee Carson, Kristina Knight, Merri McDonagh and Liz Logan for their continued support over the years.

To Flo, my fabulous editor, for believing in this story and making me dance for joy on the beach after The Call.

To my good friend Caroline—who will probably never read this—thank you for giving me the space and time to write.

Lastly, to Tom. You know why.

CHAPTER ONE

CONNOR PRESTON COULDN'T believe his eyes. She was sitting on his bed in the moonlight, brazen as you like, with her slender back curved towards him. One arm propped her up, taking her weight, and her head was dipped, as if she were posing for one of those romance book covers he'd seen in the airport newsagents.

He guessed she'd just got out of the shower, because her long blonde hair hung in wet clumps around her shoulders. He watched in irritation as a water droplet ran down the shadowed line of her spine before dripping onto his bedspread.

Through his travel-weary eyes she seemed to cast a glow in front of her, as if all the cloying positivity she used to force on him day after day radiated from her.

Katherine Meers.

He'd thought he'd finally convinced her it was over between them, but here she was, waiting naked in his bed again, in his holiday home. A holiday home that he couldn't remember ever telling her about. Was nowhere a safe haven from her needy optimism?

'What the hell are you doing in my bed, Katherine?' He knew his voice was gruff and unfriendly—nothing like the laid-back drawl he'd cultivated over the years—

but he was tired and grumpy and not in the mood for another showdown with his stalker ex-girlfriend.

But even that didn't explain the way she reacted.

Her scream was so loud he thought he felt his eardrums perforating. Her whole body jerked in fright and something gleamed momentarily in a wide arc in front of her, before raining down onto the bed with a worryingly loud *splat*.

Hair flying, she twisted round towards him and he caught a tantalising flash of her pert breasts—which were rather larger than he remembered—before she grabbed the towel that pooled around her waist and whipped it up around her.

Gazing at her shocked face in the pale glow of the moonlight, he realised he'd made a mistake.

This wasn't Katherine.

This was an altogether different problem.

Josie's heart slammed against her chest as adrenaline ricocheted through her body. After staring at her laptop in the dark for the past ten minutes she had to work hard to get her eyes to focus on the looming shape in front of her. She could barely make out the features of the enormous man standing at the foot of the bed, but she'd swear she could feel his anger.

'What do you want?' It was a reflex question—one she wasn't sure she wanted to hear the answer to—and it came out as a shaky whisper.

'I *want* my bed.' His voice was quieter this time, not exactly friendly, but there was a hint of bemusement mixed in with the exasperation.

Confusion engulfed her. Perhaps she was dreaming? The situation was certainly bizarre enough to be one of her dreams.

'What do you mean *your* bed? Who the hell are you? You scared the crap out of me.'

The man took a pace backwards in response to her rankled tone and raised his hands, palms forward. Surrender.

'Look, I'm sorry for scaring you.' His voice softened. 'I thought you were...' He paused. 'Someone else.'

Josie's eyes were slowly becoming accustomed to the dark as her night vision improved. She watched as the tension left his body. Perhaps he wasn't going to attack her, but she inched closer to her bedside lamp just in case, her muscles tight with anxiety.

She was distracted for a moment by the tinny sound of her music, playing through the earphones that had prevented her hearing his approach—which were now lying discarded on the bed.

Wrenching her attention back, she asked, 'So who are you?' forcing more authority into her voice this time, in an attempt to take control of the situation.

Perhaps if she could convince him she was in charge he might leave her alone. She'd heard somewhere that when cornered the best type of defence was attack. Although her only actual experience of being attacked was fighting for funding for the business—facing down aggressively assertive venture capitalists—which was not the same thing as a midnight stand-off with a strange man.

'Connor Preston. I own this place,' he said.

Josie blew out a small sigh, her heart-rate slowing a fraction. Preston. Okay. He must be Abigail's brother—the wanderer—returning home from a life living off his trust fund. He wasn't what she'd expected at all. Abigail was the total opposite of her brother: petite and willowy. This man was anything but petite. It was hard to gauge from her position in the bed, but she'd guess he was at least six foot four and built like an ox. *Not* the sort of vision you wanted to encounter alone in the middle of the night.

'Who are *you*?' The gruff timbre of his voice coming at her through the gloom was unnerving.

She leant across and switched on the bedside light. Yup, he was big, all right, and rugged and unshaven. His dark blond hair looked as if it could do with a cut and his clothes were creased and unkempt. He looked exhausted; his eyes dull with fatigue. Based on what Abigail had told her, she guessed he must be in his early thirties—only a few years older than her—but he looked as though he'd lived through every second of them. He had a strong face—not classically handsome, but definitely arresting. The type of man who would always be noticed, no matter where he was or who he was with.

Her skin prickled as he scrutinised her in return and a hot flush travelled through her body, leaving a sizzling pulse in the most unnerving places.

'I'm Abigail's business partner. Josie Marchpane,' she said, aware her voice was somewhat squeakier than normal. She waited for a sign of recognition on his face. It didn't come; he just stared back, assessing her. 'Abi said I could stay here for a while....' She tailed off as his expression grew darker.

'Is that right?' His tone was abrupt now, and unfriendly.

There was a heavy silence in the room as they looked at each other.

Silence?

Something was wrong.

The music had stopped playing. With horror, Josie suddenly realised that, in the shock of Connor's appearance she'd forgotten about the drink she'd thrown all over the bed...and her laptop.

Twisting round, she looked down to see the screen had gone black. When she tapped the space bar, then jabbed all the other buttons in panic, nothing happened.

It looked as if her laptop hadn't agreed with being showered with juice, and had died in disgust.

'No, no, no, no, *no*!' All the work she'd done since she'd got here was on that machine. She'd stupidly assumed there would be an internet connection, so she could back her work up, but that had been another surprise that Abi hadn't warned her about. Deliberately. She was sure of it.

'What's wrong?'

Connor's deep drawl broke into her consciousness. She'd almost forgotten him in her panic.

'I just killed my computer with orange juice.' It would have been funny if it wasn't so absolutely devastating. Losing her laptop was tantamount to losing her right hand.

'Orange juice?' He nodded slowly. 'So that's what you've christened my bed with.'

Irritation got the better of her. How could he be concerned about the state of the bed when her laptop had kicked the bucket?

'I've just lost three days' worth of work.'

He appeared unfazed by her snippy tone. 'Do you always work naked?' Crossing his arms and raising an eyebrow, he gave her a look that bordered on seductive.

The hairs on her arms stood up in response and heat burned in her belly. Acutely aware of her nakedness under the towel, she broke eye contact and looked around for her clothes. She'd have to walk past him to get to them. That meant skirting the end of the bed and passing within a foot of him. The thought made her uneasy and a little tick throbbed in her eye.

Rubbing a hand over her face, she tried to wipe away the befuddling mix of sensations. 'I was in the shower and I had a thought.' Her voice trembled and she cleared her throat to relieve the tightness.

He tilted his head in an approximation of bewildered understanding.

She sighed. 'I'm writing a tender document for work and I was hit with inspiration. I didn't want to forget it before I had a chance to write it down.'

'I get it,' he said, giving a bemused shake of his head.

Good God, he knew how to get under her skin.

'Look, do you mind?' She forced her shoulders back and tipped up her chin. 'I'm not exactly prepared for socialising right now. Can we talk about this in the morning?'

Connor dragged his gaze up from where her fingers grasped the towel and frowned. 'Where am I supposed to sleep? You've taken the only bed.'

'Try the sofa.'

The look on his face almost made her laugh.

'I've been travelling for three months. I was looking forward to finally sleeping in my own bed.'

'If I'd known you were coming we could have worked something out,' she retorted.

'Worked something out, huh?' He dropped his gaze down her body, taking in the swell of her figure that the towel barely concealed.

The disturbing throb began again, deep inside her. She pulled the towel tighter, unnerved by his attention. It was disconcerting being half-naked in front of a total stranger. Especially one as unsettling as Connor Preston.

'You know what I mean,' she said, nerves making her

tone snappy again. The heavy unease she'd been wrestling with for the past week stretched its tentacles. She blew out a steadying breath, counted to three. 'Look, can we sleep on it tonight and work it out in the morning? I doubt you want to sleep in a damp, orange-soaked bed anyway, right?' She cocked what she hoped would come across as an affable smile.

He continued to size her up for a moment. 'Okay,' he said slowly, then ran a hand over his tired eyes. 'I've been travelling all day and I haven't got the energy to deal with this now. I'll sleep on the sofa tonight. We'll talk in the morning.'

He turned abruptly and left the room, slamming the door behind him and leaving her shaky and bewildered.

Josie woke late the next morning.

After failing to resuscitate her laptop she'd scribbled down as much as she could remember from the tender document, trying not to let panic sink its teeth into her, before falling into a fitful sleep. Her senses had been on high alert following the run-in with Connor, and every creak and groan in the old property had made her jump. She'd finally dropped off just as the birds started their dawn chorus, exhaustion winning the battle over her adrenalised body.

She lay staring at the ceiling, cursing her bad luck. It hadn't been the best few weeks ever and it didn't look as though things were about to improve any time soon. Hopefully her computer would dry out and boot up again in a few hours, so she wouldn't have to spend the next week reconstructing the whole document. If not—well, she'd have to find a repair shop somewhere and see if it was salvageable. More delays. Just what she didn't need. Just what the *business* didn't need.

And she had another problem now. Abigail's brother was obviously annoyed to find someone else using his house—which was understandable; if she'd come home to find someone in her bed she'd have been totally thrown too—but she'd promised Abi that she'd have a proper break away after the whole humiliating debacle at work.

If only she hadn't lost her cool and flipped out like that in front of everyone perhaps Abi would have taken her worries about the state of the business more seriously. She'd ended up looking like a total loon.

No wonder her business partner had been so firm about her staying here for a couple of weeks—in her words 'to give everyone a chance to calm down and work things through'—and she hadn't wanted to argue and strain their precarious relationship further. Agreeing to a couple of weeks here had seemed like a sensible compromise, but Connor wanting this place too had thrown a spanner in the works. She really didn't need the hassle of finding some faceless hotel to stay in during peak season. Anyway, this place was just as much Abi's as Connor's, and *she'd* arrived here first.

With newfound determination she tossed back the covers and slipped out of bed, pausing for a moment to luxuriate in the feel of her toes digging into the soft Persian rug before going to the antique wardrobe to find some clothes. Grabbing a pair of jeans and a loose T-shirt, she pulled them on, then stripped the king-sized brass bed, bundling up the sheets ready to stick in the washing machine.

When she'd arrived a few days ago she'd been blown away by the beauty of the place. She'd expected a run-down holiday home in the middle of nowhere. Instead she'd found a characterful farmhouse a twenty-minute drive from Aix-en-Provence.

It had a large kitchen diner and a cosy, snug down-stairs, complete with battered leather sofas and an old wood-burning stove. The air smelt delicious—like herbs and woodsmoke and sunshine. Nothing like the sanitised holiday lets her mother had used to scour with foul-smelling disinfectant when they first arrived on their interminable family vacations. Upstairs there was a large bathroom with an enormous claw-footed bath and a separate shower cubicle, along with a beautiful antique vanity unit. Worryingly, she remembered, of the three bedrooms only one was furnished: the one she was currently sleeping in. The others looked as though they were being used to store various strangely shaped equipment and large crates of goodness only knew what.

So only one bed.

She needed to talk to Abigail's brother and find out his plans. Then, if he meant to stay, gently persuade him to change them. Or maybe not so gently, if it came to that. The last thing she needed was someone asking questions and spoiling her fragile peace. She was going to do her time here, prove to Abi that she was fit and rested enough to come back to work, then get on with advancing the business.

She was used to hard bargaining at work; compared to that, this ought to be a relatively easy battle to win.

Glancing at herself in the mirror, she was confronted with a scary sight. Her normally immaculate sweep of blonde hair was mussed and sticking out at odd angles after she'd slept on it wet and she had dark circles under her eyes.

Once she'd pulled a brush through her hair and tied it back in a tight bun she splashed her face with cold, reviving water from the white porcelain sink in the room. That would have to do for now. First breakfast, then a shower, then a confrontation with Connor Preston.

Descending the stairs, she was hit by the tantalising aromas of fresh coffee and bacon.

He was up already.

There was a mound of mud-splattered bags at the door and a pair of large hiking boots leant haphazardly against the wall in the hallway.

What big feet you have, Mr Preston.

Her memory of him was blurry this morning, as if she'd dreamed him.

No such luck.

He was standing at the stove with his back to her, but as she moved quietly into the kitchen he turned around. Her insides lurched as they made eye contact.

'Good morning. I trust you found my bed comfortable?'

His voice was a low rumble, but a little friendlier than the previous night. And, yup, he was just as impressive as she remembered. An unwelcome tingle tickled the base of her spine.

Think of it as a business negotiation, Josie. Do not let him charm you. You are a strong, capable woman. Take control.

'Yes, thanks,' she replied lightly. She would *not* apologise for not budging last night. She didn't want him to get the impression she was some sort of sappy push-over and lose any advantage she might have.

He gestured towards a seat at the table with a lazy flick of his hand. 'Sit. I'll get us some breakfast and we'll talk.'

His commanding tone rankled, but she ignored it and took the seat opposite him, straightening her spine and leaning into the table, ready to fight her corner. She needed to choose her battles wisely here.

He had quite a presence. A big man, with a natural strength and a broad build, he certainly looked powerful, but not pumped up like a boxer or a body-builder. Intimidating.

She wasn't used to feeling dwarfed. Her six-foot frame usually afforded her a sense of authority, but she wasn't feeling the power of it with him around.

He took a break from stirring the eggs to run a hand through his shaggy blond hair, swiping the fringe out of his eyes. Something about this simple action sent a frisson of excitement through her. What the hell was wrong with her? Clearly she hadn't had enough sleep. She laced her fingers together under the table to stop them twitching in her lap.

In a daze, she watched him pour coffee into large earthenware mugs and pile bacon and scrambled eggs onto plates. After sliding them onto the table he sat opposite her and began to shovel food into his mouth without even glancing her way.

It took him less than two minutes to clear his plate, and afterwards he leant back in his chair and waited patiently for her to finish. Josie could feel his gaze burning into her skin, but forced her eyes to look down at her plate, willing her hand to stay steady as she forked eggs into her mouth.

Finally, pushing her plate away, she picked up her coffee and looked at him. He continued to observe her without breaking his gaze. She could sense the force of his will, digging away at her defences. He clearly didn't want her company any more than she wanted his.

Her heart played in quick time against her chest, but she didn't look away.

This must be the way he wins his battles, Josie thought. *By silent intimidation.* He'd just wait for her to break and say she'd leave. She'd come across this strategy before at work. Being a woman in a high-powered position meant she had to deal with this kind of resistance a lot, and she'd become pretty good at fielding it, so instead of looking away she stared right back.

His eyes were an attention-grabbing ice-blue, ringed with graphite-grey, and the intensity in his gaze almost broke her.

Not today, matey.

After what felt like an age Connor placed his mug back on the table and allowed a slow smile to spread across his face. At once his rugged features came alive: his eyes lit with warmth and the sharp angles of his face softened, making him seem younger, more playful and somehow more human. It was a deliciously sexy sight.

Her whole body trembled as a surge of lust blindsided her and hot coffee slopped over the rim of the mug onto her lap.

Damn it.

Gritting her teeth, she ignored the burning sensation as the liquid soaked into her jeans, hoping he hadn't noticed.

His smile morphed into a quizzical frown. 'You okay? That must have stung.'

'I'm fine,' she muttered, putting her mug carefully onto the table before she did any more damage to herself.

He took advantage of her weakened state to launch his attack. 'So, Josie, when are you leaving?'

His tone was even, as if he were making polite conversation, but she felt the power behind the words. Oh, he was good, all right.

Drawing her shoulders back, she gave him her fully-in-control face before answering, noting with satisfaction that he'd leant further back in his chair and broken eye contact, dipping his gaze to somewhere below her neck.

'In a week or two. Abigail offered this place to me and I accepted in good faith.' She looked at him hard, determined to keep it together. 'I haven't had a holiday for three years and she thought I could do with the break.'

That was understating the facts a little, but there was no way she was admitting the whole truth to him. She was too proud. Plus, it was none of his damn business.

He rubbed his hand over his eyes, obviously still tired after travelling and then sleeping on the less than mansized sofa.

She actually felt her insides softening. 'Look, I know this is your place, and you probably want to relax in peace, but you can't just kick me out.' She jabbed a finger at him. 'This house is just as much Abigail's as yours, and you weren't supposed to be coming back any time soon. Why didn't you let her know?'

He leant in towards her and she couldn't help but move away from the overwhelming force of his sudden proximity. 'I don't answer to anyone—especially not my damn sister.' He tapped his finger hard on the table. 'She knows this is where I base myself when I'm not travelling, she never comes here, and I don't see why I should put up with her waifs and strays when the whim takes her.'

His voice was low and steady, all cool control and understated power, but she refused to be scared off.

'I'm not a waif *or* a stray, and I'm not going anywhere.' She crossed her arms and bit down hard on her lip. His eyes dropped to her mouth and she shifted self-consciously in her seat. Blood pulsed through her veins as his eyes slowly returned to hers, his pupils large and dark against his irises.

She released her lip and rubbed her tongue over it in

response. What had made her do that? She needed to argue her case convincingly here and keep focused on her goal. Instead her body seemed intent on deliberately provoking a physical reaction out of him. This was really unlike her. She rarely flirted. She didn't have time for it.

'What do you propose I do? Sleep on the couch until you decide to leave?' he said, a smile twitching at the corner of his mouth.

She spread out her hands on the tabletop and took a steadying breath before spearing him with her sternest stare. 'As far as I understand it, Abi has as much right to this place as you do. This is supposed to be my holiday—a chance to get some peace and quiet. It's not my fault you two can't communicate properly.'

His smile faltered. 'You expect me to *leave*?'

That awful softening thing was happening again. *Ignore it, Josie. Stand firm.* 'Yes.' She waited for his response, her fingers now drumming a soft beat on the table.

'Why would I do that?' His expression was impassive.

'Because I was here first.'

He barked out a laugh. 'You're calling dibs on *my* house?'

'It's a perfectly valid negotiating technique.'

He considered her for a moment and she shifted in her chair, straightening her back in readiness for his next move.

'Do you cook?'

What the hell?

'Not unless you count microwaving ready meals or sloshing milk over cereal.'

Connor raised his eyebrows. 'I don't.'

She crossed her arms. 'Then, no, I don't cook.'

Connor gave her a questioning look and she flushed under his scrutiny.

She shrugged, fighting the heat of her discomfort. 'My job's demanding. The last thing I want to do when I get in is cook.'

'Really? I find it relaxing.'

His eyes searched her face and her skin heated in response.

'What do you do to relax?'

There was a hint of reproach in his expression as his gaze locked with hers. She shifted in her chair, looking away from him. Why was he making her feel so uncomfortable? She had nothing to be ashamed about.

'I go to the gym sometimes.' She racked her brain, trying to find something to impress him with, but nothing came to mind.

Connor shook his head slowly, radiating disapproval, but his expression softened as he leant in closer to her. The hairs on the back of her neck lifted in response and her heart pummelled her chest as his gaze roved her face before dropping to her lips.

'I'm sure we can think of some way to work this out.'

His voice was low and the double meaning was not lost on her. He stood suddenly, pushing his chair away from the table and grabbing their plates, turning to dump them next to the sink. He stilled, staring down at the counter, before turning back. There was a challenge in his expression now.

'You can cut my hair.'

Josie blinked at him in surprise, her body a tangle of confusion and lust. What was he doing to her? The mixture of forceful self-confidence and provocative teasing was disorientating her, turning her insides to mulch and her brain to jelly.

'Did you say you want me to cut your hair?'

'Yes.'

She gave him a stunned smile. 'What's wrong with going to a hairdresser?'

'A waste of money. Anyway, I'm not losing a morning driving to Aix just to get a haircut. I'm sick of it hanging in my face—you just need to chop a couple of inches off all round. Then I'll be ready to face the world.'

Relaxing her arms, she dropped her hands into her lap and tapped her fingers together. 'If I do it will you let me have the house?'

He shrugged. 'Depends on how good a job you do.'

She snorted. 'What if I make a mess of it?'

'I'm trusting you not to. Come on, Josie, it's not rocket science. You know the general principle, right? Look, I can't get my fingers in those piddly little nail scissors, and the only other sharp things I have in this house are the kitchen knives and the garden shears.'

'I may end up needing those. It looks like you've been washing your hair with engine oil.'

That tantalising smile played about his lips again and her stomach flipped over.

'Yeah, well, it's tough finding a power shower in the middle of a rainforest.'

He flicked his hair out of his eyes with those long, strong-looking fingers and her hands did a nervous sort of skitter in her lap. What would it feel like to be in such close proximity to that powerful frame and all that hard muscle? Blood rushed straight between her legs, causing a hard ache there, and before she could stop herself she rocked forward in the chair to try and relieve the pressure.

Clearing her throat to dislodge the strangling tension, she tore her gaze away from him to scan the kitchen cupboards, the dresser, the patio doors—anywhere but his irresistible body—while her heart thumped against her chest. She needed to stand up and move around before she started rutting the chair. What the hell was going on with her crazy body?

'So where are these scissors, then?'

He was smiling when she looked back at him and the victory on his face made her frown. How had he managed to talk her into this? But then what the hell? If that was what it took to get rid of him, so be it. She'd never been one to walk away from a challenge. She'd also never cut hair in her life. Still, it wasn't her problem if he ended up looking as if a child had got busy with the scissors while he was asleep. Maybe she should make a mess of it just to pay him back for that supercilious expression.

Despite being rather taken with the idea, she knew she wouldn't. She was too much of a good girl, and she wanted him gone.

'They're in the middle drawer of the dresser,' he said, nodding towards the grand piece of furniture at the back of the kitchen.

'Okay. You get them and I'll grab a towel.'

He gave her a quizzical look, but there was a twinkle of mischief in his eyes. 'You want me in just a towel for this?'

From his expression she guessed he was quite taken with the idea, and her insides twisted in a strange, excited sort of way.

'That won't be necessary. It's to keep the hair off your clothes,' she said through oddly numb lips.

'You're the boss,' he said, getting up and striding over to the dresser.

She legged it out of the kitchen and up the stairs, taking her time to find the oldest-looking towel out of the linen cupboard and sucking in deep breaths until she felt composed enough to be in the same room with him again. At least he'd be leaving after this, she told herself, ignoring a niggle of disappointment that came out of nowhere. She needed alone time right now.

Right?

Returning to the kitchen, she found he'd dragged a chair into the middle of the floor and was seated, waiting patiently for her to get back.

'Not too much off the top,' he said as she approached him and laid the towel gently over his wide shoulders.

It wasn't long enough to meet across his chest and after a moment of fussing with it she left it to hang there.

God, the size of him.

She wasn't going to have to bend down far to get on a level with his head. Nerves jumping, she picked up the scissors and tentatively ran her hands through his mop of hair, gauging the best place to start.

He groaned gently in response and she almost jumped away in fright.

'I can already tell you've got magic hands,' he said.

From the tone of his voice he was clearly enjoying winding her up, and she kicked herself for allowing him to make her so jittery. Putting her fingers back into his hair, she pulled it harder this time, in an attempt to show him who was in charge.

He chuckled: a low, seductive sound that made her mouth water.

Flipping heck, Josie, pull it together.

After taking a first tentative snip—and finding it actually seemed to look okay—she worked her way around his head, cutting the top first, to reveal the smooth, darker underside of his hair.

Heat rose from his scalp as she worked and her stiff fingers warmed up, allowing her to cut faster. She pictured her own hairdresser, Lenny, and focused on what he did when cutting her hair, working her way carefully.

It felt odd not to talk while she worked, and the silence lay thick and heavy in the large kitchen. What the hell was she supposed to talk about? What would Lenny do?

Make small talk. You can do that, right? Just say something, Josie. Anything.

'You know, you look nothing like I expected,' she said.

'No?' His voice was infused with amusement.

'You're so…' She willed her addled brain to come up with any word except the one fighting to get out.

She lost.

'Big.'

He turned to catch her eye and she looked away quickly, so as not to get sucked into flirty banter with him—not when she was so close she could inhale the minty aroma of his toothpaste and the dark undertones of whatever product he used on his body that made him smell so—what was the word? *Appetising…*

Thank God for the soothing action of lifting and snipping at his hair. Mercifully, it helped her maintain focus, although her cool was shot to pieces.

'Judging by your complexion and the size of your frame I'm guessing there's some Scandinavian blood in there somewhere?' she barrelled on.

'Icelandic.'

'I'd never have guessed that from your sister—she's so dark. Hair *and* complexion.' Okay, this was good. Well, better. Sort of…

'She got the French blood.'

'On your mother's side?' *Lift, pull, snip.*

'Yeah, my paternal grandmother was French. This was her home. She left it to me and Abi when she died.'

There was a change in his posture and a new tension

in his jaw that made her wonder what he'd omitted from that statement. A memory of Abi telling her their grandmother was the only person Connor had ever cared about swam into her mind.

She paused, not quite sure how to frame her next question. 'Abi says she hasn't seen you in a long time?'

His head moved up a notch as his shoulders stiffened. 'No.'

She waited for him to elucidate but the silence stretched on.

'I think she'd like to see you sometime.'

'Hmm…'

She'd hit a conversational roadblock. Another approach, maybe? 'So what keeps you so busy?'

'I travel a lot.' His tone was dismissive, as if he were closing down this conversation too.

Don't give up, Josie.

'You've just got back from somewhere?'

'South America. I'm leaving for India in a few days.'

Abi hadn't told her much about Connor—only that he was always on the move and never came to England to see her. They'd been on a rare night out and three cocktails down when she'd talked about him. There had been a heavy sadness to her tone, and an unhappy resignation to his snubbing of her. His name hadn't been mentioned since and Josie had tactfully avoided mentioning him again.

From Abi's description of him she'd expected a self-aggrandising playboy with power issues—not this challenging, provocative giant of a man.

Moving round to the front of him, she made sure to keep looking only at the long fringe of hair left to cut. The heat of his gaze burned her skin as she shuffled between his spread thighs to get close enough to reach in.

With shaking hands she took hold of the front of it, the backs of her fingers gently brushing the warm skin of his forehead. His heat invaded her and she experienced a whole body flush which concentrated into a core of molten lava in the depths of her pelvis. She wished her hair wasn't pulled back so severely so she could hide her fiery face in the safety of its protective curtain.

After snipping at the length of hair until she was satisfied, she took a step back away from his weird vortex-like pull and dropped the scissors onto the kitchen table.

'You're done.'

He was looking at her with a curious expression. 'You know, there's something very familiar about you.'

Dammit. Just when she'd thought she'd got away with it. She really didn't want to talk about her sister right now.

She shrugged. 'I have one of those faces. You've never met me before.' He seemed satisfied with this answer, thank goodness, and threw her a quick nod.

Pulling off the towel, he dropped it onto the floor. 'How does it look?'

Meeting his gaze, she willed her cheeks to deflame. 'Actually, it looks pretty good.' She was oddly pleased with how successful a cut it was, considering she'd never done it before in her life.

He nodded, releasing his slow grin, then turned abruptly and walked out of the room and up the stairs— she guessed to check his new haircut for himself.

Grateful for this small reprieve, she grabbed a dustpan and brush from under the sink and swept up the hair that had landed on the floor, her body humming with alien sensations. She hoped to goodness her face would return to some kind of normal colour by the time he got back.

She'd cleared up every bit of hair and made herself

another drink by the time he returned, his face now scrupulously clean-shaven.

What a transformation. All her blood dashed south to pulse wildly between her thighs as she took in his new, clean-cut appearance. He'd pulled his shorn hair into messy spikes, and now his bristles weren't obscuring it his bone structure seemed ridiculously and beautifully chiselled. He was the picture of pure, healthy, brute strength.

'Okay. So we're good here,' he said, apparently unaware of the catastrophic effect he was having on her. 'You've earned your right to stay.'

Sucking in a deep breath, she attempted to jump-start her brain into functioning. 'So that's it? Negotiation over? You're leaving?'

He laughed and stepped closer to her. She took half a step back before checking herself.

Hold steady there, Josie.

'You're not getting rid of me that easily. You seem to be a useful sort of person to have around. I'm only going to be here for a few days, but I'll take the sofa since you won dibs.'

Before she had a chance to protest he spun round, pulling open the patio doors and exiting onto the terrace, shouting, 'Dinner at eight!' over his shoulder as he strode away.

CHAPTER TWO

AFTER MAKING HIS sharp exit Connor wandered down to the bottom of the farmhouse's land and along the perimeter. In front of him the sun-washed landscape throbbed with colour, the vibrant greens and yellows of the rapeseed crops standing stark against the sea of lavender in fields that stretched for miles. In the distance chalky white mountains broke against the azure-blue of the sky.

It was his idea of heaven on earth.

He loved this place. It felt as far away from reality as you could get. That appealed to him. That and the simplicity of it.

He leant on the wooden fence and assessed what had just happened.

Josie Marchpane was seriously disturbing, that was for sure. He wasn't easily impressed, but this woman—oh, man, did she have something. There was something familiar about her too, but he couldn't put his finger on it and that bothered him.

When he'd found out she was here at Abigail's invitation his instinct had been to try and get rid of her as quickly as possible. He wasn't interested in ever seeing his self-serving sister again, and even less willing to entertain one of her friends in his house. But the more he'd talked to Josie, the more he'd come to like her. She didn't buckle easily and he respected that.

Despite the dark circles under her eyes and the ghostly pallor she was hot. It wasn't the delicate contours of her heart-shaped face that got to him, or even the endless expanse of leg hiding beneath those expensive-looking jeans. It was her almond-shaped hazel eyes that flashed with fire when she was on the defensive. He wasn't used to being stood up to, let alone put in his place, and he found he kind of liked it.

He knew he had an effect on her too, no matter how hard she was trying to disguise it. It was visible in the flare of her pupils and the flush of colour on her cheeks; in the way her body turned towards him even when she fought against it. It would be hard to convince her mind to submit to him, but not her body.

He hadn't needed her to cut his hair—he could have quite easily visited a barber the following day—but he'd wanted to see if he could get her to do it. He'd been in a playful mood and it had amused him—until she'd been right there, touching him, invading his space and warming his skin with her nervous heat. Then he'd realised it had been an excuse to get closer to her. He'd wanted to know whether she smelled as good as she looked and he hadn't been disappointed.

The fact that she'd risen to his challenge despite her initial reticence intrigued him. She hadn't been able to resist it.

He recognised an urge on his part to break through her carefully constructed wall of cool just for the satisfaction of melting her. He craved it. Just as he'd craved coming back here, to the one place that felt vaguely like home. It wouldn't be long until he'd had his fill of sitting still, but at the moment it was necessary—imperative, even.

That was why he couldn't pick up and stay at a hotel for the few days he had left before his next project started. He'd been aware of an unusual yearning for this place for the past few weeks, as if it had called to him. Something akin to nostalgia, or what he thought that might feel like; he'd never experienced it before. Usually he actively moved *away* from the past.

Wandering back up to the house, he parked himself on a lounger on the terrace and leant back, willing his overworked muscles to relax. He needed this peace and calm and nothingness for a few days before he rejoined the hurricane of his life.

The bathroom window above him slammed shut, jarring him out of his relaxing state and setting his teeth on edge. She must be about to take a shower. The thought of hot water sluicing over that curvaceous body and those heavy, rounded breasts was enough to give him an erection.

The trouble was, the last thing he needed right now was another woman problem. It had been soul-destroying breaking up with Katherine and persuading her he wasn't the right guy to make her happy, then spending months avoiding her angry, pleading phone calls and sudden appearances out of the blue. She didn't understand that the lifestyle he'd chosen wasn't conducive to settling in one place and playing house. It had been an exhausting time. He was afraid that even a short, sharp affair now could leach the remaining life out of him, and he needed his mojo intact if he was going to keep the momentum of his projects going.

But it didn't mean he couldn't have fun playing with Josie. He'd be out of here in a few days, so what harm could it do to spend a bit of time figuring her out? There had to be more to her story than she was letting on. She didn't seem like the kind of woman who could fritter away two weeks in the middle of nowhere. She had a nervous sort of energy about her that gave the impression she had more important things to be doing than just sitting and relaxing.

He wanted to know why.

She'd been well and truly had and it didn't feel good.

Josie squeezed shampoo hard into her hand and thumped the bottle down onto the shower shelf in her anger. How could she have allowed him to talk her into embarrassing herself like that? She was clearly off her game because she was tired and stressed about the business. There was no way he would have tricked her like that ordinarily. In retrospect, she wished she'd given him a bald spot and an extra short fringe, just so she'd have something to mollify her.

What was she going to do now? He clearly wasn't going to budge easily. She'd have to make as much of a nuisance of herself as possible and hope he'd get fed up and decide he'd be better off somewhere else.

She could phone Abi and explain the situation, of course, but she didn't want it to look as though she couldn't fight her own battles. And her business partner had enough on her plate as it was.

Shutting off the shower, she stepped carefully out of the tray and towelled herself dry.

The pile of dirty clothes on the floor gave her an idea.

After dressing in a light floral sundress, and drying off her hair so it swung around her shoulders, she gathered up her dirty laundry and dumped it on the bed, ready to take downstairs. Her laptop was sitting on the window-sill, where she'd left it in the hope that the sun would help dry it out, and she went over and tapped the power button again, praying that it would suddenly spring to life.

No dice.

A sharp pain throbbed in her skull and she massaged the sides of her forehead to try and relieve the pressure.

'Join me for a drink on the terrace?'

She jumped at the sound of Connor's deep voice, twisting round to see him slouched against the doorjamb of the bedroom. He filled the doorway with his immense physique.

'I got the impression you wanted me to keep out of your way,' she answered, nonchalantly flicking her hair over her shoulder. She wasn't going to show him how nervy she was around him. All she had right now was her self-control, and she was damned if she was going to let that slip away from her too.

'I changed my mind. I could do with some company and you could do with some sun.' His gaze rested on her pale shoulders. 'Do you spend *any* time outside?'

Truthfully, she didn't tend to spend much time outdoors. She'd been too busy with work and had often ended up working at weekends to keep up with her heavy workload. She couldn't remember the last time she'd just sat in the sunshine.

'The sun's very damaging to your skin, you know. You'll be old before your time.' She pointed towards his tanned forearms in a vain attempt to shut him up.

He smiled. 'Full of vitamin D, though. Good for your happiness levels.'

Before she had time to reply, he pushed himself away from the doorway and disappeared.

After a few moments of arguing with herself about the wisdom of spending more time in his vicinity she grabbed her dirty clothes and a pen and notebook and went down to the kitchen. She shoved her clothes in the washing machine, set it going, then sauntered outside to find Connor reclining on a lounger, his shirt discarded on the floor next to him.

Great.

Josie stared. She couldn't help it. His body was… well…*divine*. That skin—the glorious tanned sleekness of it. The way it undulated over the muscles of his stomach and stretched over the peaks of his collarbones. The broadness of his shoulders made her think of a superhero with their almost obscene size. She'd never seen such a magnificent body in the flesh.

Cue whole body flush.

Tearing her eyes away, she sat on the lounger next to him, barely managing to control her limbs.

He turned to look at her, a crooked smile playing about his lips as if he sensed her discomfort. 'Help yourself to a drink.' He gestured towards a jug of iced fruit juice and a couple of tumblers on a small table between them.

She eyed it suspiciously. 'I'm not thirsty, thanks.' She didn't entirely trust him. There was something odd about him suddenly wanting her company, but she couldn't quite put her finger on why it felt so dangerous to be out here with him. She didn't for a second think he would hurt her, but it was unnerving all the same.

Dropping her notebook casually onto the table between them, she shuffled about on the lounger to try and get comfy. When she glanced up at him, he seemed to be sizing her up.

She raised a questioning eyebrow at him, fighting the urge to look away from his evaluating stare.

'You work a lot, right?'

She sat up straighter, warming up for what she was

sure was about to be some sort of scrap. 'My job keeps me pretty busy.'

'Thought so. You have that computer crouch people get when they work at a desk too much. The only time you set your shoulders back and push that magnificent rack at me is when you're facing me down over something.'

How was she supposed to respond to *that* little gem? By playing it cool.

'I don't suppose you come across many desks on your *jaunts* around the world.'

He broke eye contact to pick up the jug of iced juice and pour himself a shot into one of the glasses. 'You'd be surprised what I *come* across,' he said, in that low, seductive voice of his.

The hairs stood up on the back of her neck again and she snort-laughed in response, blood rushing straight to her face in embarrassment at the awful noise she'd made. Picking up the jug from where he'd set it down, she concentrated on pouring herself some juice to hide her humiliation. The ice clinked in her glass as she held it unsteadily in her hand, so she rested it on her knee instead.

Connor lay back, linking his fingers together behind his head, a smile playing about his lips. He knew exactly what he was doing to her and he clearly loved seeing her squirm. *Bastard.*

A minute went by before he spoke again. 'What do you do that keeps you shackled to a desk?'

'*Shackled?* Interesting choice of word.' She didn't dare look him in the face in case he saw how much she was floundering.

'The imagery pleases me.'

He turned in the lounger to face her and her gaze was magnetically drawn to his toned torso. It was unnerving, being faced with a sight like that whilst trying to maintain a polite line of conversation.

'You have a vivid imagination,' she said.

'It's a prerequisite. I spend a lot of time alone.'

She really needed to get the conversation back on safe ground. 'We provide software solutions for marketing and research departments.'

'That must be fascinating.'

His tone was so dry she felt like dousing him with her ice-cold drink.

'It took us three years to build the business to this point and we're proud of what we've achieved.'

'Good for you.'

He totally didn't mean a word of it.

Ignore him, Josie, the guy's a loser.

Grabbing her notebook and pen from where she'd dropped them on the table, she turned deliberately away from him and began to make some notes, forcing his presence out of her mind.

'What are you writing?'

Apparently he didn't like to be ignored. 'I'm trying to reconstruct my tender document.'

He frowned. 'I thought you were supposed to be on holiday?'

Josie shuffled uncomfortably on the lounger. 'I am, but I'm making a head start for when I get back. I was doing pretty well until my laptop died.' She gave him a pointed stare.

Connor let out a snort. 'I can't believe you brought a laptop on holiday. No wonder you're so…' He waved his hand in a loose flapping motion at her.

'So what?'

'I don't know…edgy.'

'I'm not edgy.' She flicked her hair over her shoulder and scowled at him. 'I'm diligent.'

'Really? So you're *not* heading off to the nearest computer repair shop later, so you can get right back to work before your head explodes.' He mimed the explosion he was obviously picturing in his mind.

'You're funny. You know that? You're a very *funny* man.'

'I'm right, though, aren't I? I bet you can't stand to be without it for one day.'

'Don't be ridiculous. Of course I can.' She ignored the stutter in her heartbeat and leant back in the chair, gazing up at the slow-moving clouds above her. Her body was drenched in sweat. Had a heat wave descended?

Connor just grunt-laughed in response.

She chose to ignore him.

'Can't somebody else write your document?'

After pausing, she chose her answer carefully. 'They're working on it at the moment, but I'm the one who has the most experience in writing these things.'

'So you don't trust anyone else to do the job?'

Sighing, she put her fingers together, tip to tip, and waited for the irritation to subside. 'If I don't work on it now I'm going to have to do it when I get back—edit what the team's done, that is—which will only allow minimal time to get it up to scratch before the deadline.'

'And you're sure they won't be able to handle it without you?'

'Based on experience—no.'

He nodded slowly, looking at her intently as if waiting for something more.

'Why are you looking at me like that?'

'Like what?' He was all innocence.

'You don't believe me?'

He shrugged. 'I'm not saying that. I was just wondering why you hired your staff if you don't trust them to
do their jobs properly.'

She really didn't want to be talking about this. She
was hyper-aware of the underlying panic, humming just
below the surface, which she'd been struggling to suppress for weeks.

'We can't afford to get anything wrong right now. It's
a tough marketplace.' She hoped the brusqueness of her
tone would stop him asking any more about it.

'So it's all work and no play for you, right?'

His expression was neutral. She couldn't tell whether
he was teasing her.

Either way, Josie felt her blood begin to boil. How dare
he? He didn't even know her. He had no right to make
judgements on her like that. She'd come across these
disparaging attitudes to women in high-powered jobs
so frequently that hers was a natural response by now.

She glared at him, her eyes narrowed. 'Just because I
work hard—and prefer not to loaf around the world on
someone else's dime,' she added pointedly, 'it doesn't
make me some hard-nosed bore. I happen to be very well
respected....' She petered out as the truth of her situation
came flooding back to her.

He looked at her with his eyebrows raised. 'I've heard
all this before. The crazy working schedule. The inability
to live outside of work. One holiday every three years...'

Josie squirmed at this.

'...the ever-diminishing social life.' He broke off to
take a sip of his drink. 'Is it really worth it?'

Was he serious? She still couldn't tell. 'Of course it's
worth it,' she said as calmly as she could. 'Anyway, it's nothing like that.' She flapped a hand at him, but the tension in
her muscles made the action jerky and over-exaggerated.

Connor looked sceptical. 'What makes it so worthwhile? Hmm? What are the benefits?'

Josie had no idea how to answer this. She had no desire to talk about what it was that drove her so hard. Not with him. Besides, she'd been doing it for so long it had become part of who she was, who she'd always been and who she always would be.

'It's about a sense of achievement. Making something great out of your life. Being respected and…and…'

She realised she was gesturing wildly at him again, like some kind of madwoman, but he'd got her blood up. She was angry at his insinuation that she was somehow making a mistake with her life choices. This was what she'd always wanted. What else could there be?

'It makes me happy,' she finished, picking up her drink and taking a long sip to cover her frustration.

'All right. I was only asking.' He held up his hands to her in mock surrender, a smile playing about his lips.

'What makes *you* such an expert anyway?' She straightened herself up on her lounger and felt her dress pull downwards, exposing more flesh than she was comfortable with. She adjusted the top hastily, then tugged the skirt back down from where it had ridden up.

Their eyes met and the air crackled between them.

'Like I say, I've seen it all before.'

His voice was low and ragged and sent chills tripping along her spine. Her head spun as she drank in his penetrating gaze.

This time it was Connor who broke eye contact first. He lay back in the recliner and gazed up at the sky, closing the subject and the unnerving connection.

Josie twisted away, lips clamped tight. What had all that been about? Maybe it had just been a fun game for him, to tease and anger her. To see how far he could push her before she snapped. Her sense of frustration increased and she had to consciously release her hands from their rigor mortis clench.

This guy was something else. He knew instinctively how to push her buttons. Well, she wasn't going to let him do it again, that was for sure.

Dumping her notebook and pen on the table, she forced herself to focus on relaxing into holiday mode to show him she was capable of doing it.

'You know, you really should put some suntan lotion on. That pale skin of yours is going to fry in this heat. You townies have no idea how to live in the sun.'

He was looking back over at her again. There wasn't a trace of the intensity that had been there a moment ago. Josie was almost relieved. At least she could deal with him when he was being overtly officious.

'There's some in the kitchen cupboard,' he added, turning away from her.

Again, his suggestion felt more like an order, but she knew he was right.

'I need to do something inside anyway,' she said, rising from the lounger and sauntering inside, determined to get her own back.

In the bathroom she took out all the products she'd been storing neatly in her washbag and scattered them around the sink and the edge of the bath, giving her emergency box of tampons pride of place on top of the toilet. After brushing her teeth again, she made sure to leave a good covering of toothpaste scum in the sink. Satisfied with the results, she returned to the kitchen, pulling her now clean clothes out of the washer and draping them all around the room. Her knickers and bra she hung right over the handle of the oven.

That would do for now.

After grabbing the bottle of suntan lotion from the

kitchen cupboard she went back outside and returned to the lounger. Taking her time, she smoothed lotion over the exposed parts of her body, then thumped the bottle down onto the table to show Connor he could leave her alone now.

He grinned at her and inclined his head. 'Want me to do your back?' he asked, a twinkle in his eye.

'No, thanks.' Just the thought of his touch disturbed her. It was too intimate an act to indulge in with him. There was no way she could handle that; she'd be a puddle on the floor. Plus, she wasn't ready to forgive him for his comments about her career.

She was so sick of people doubting her choices. Her whole life seemed to have been spent proving herself, over and over again, until she felt dizzy with it. But no way was she going to waste her time trying to explain her work ethic to someone who was plainly more than happy to let others do the hard graft while he swanned off round the world having 'experiences.'

She'd tell him that if he brought up the subject again. No more Miss Nice Girl. The guy had it coming.

She went to pick up her notepad again, then realised she was about to prove his point about not being able to stay away from working. She *could* do it. Of course she could. Her hands were only shaking because she was so irritated with him.

Right?

She wasn't planning on sunbathing out here for long, anyway. She would stay long enough to show him he couldn't intimidate her and then she'd go for a walk or something. Anything to be away from him for a while.

Connor was aware of Josie fidgeting beside him. He smiled to himself. She was obviously finding it impossible to lie still. Not that he could blame her; he'd gone at her pretty hard—but it was so much fun winding her up.

He'd been comfortably winning the conversation until she'd shifted in her chair, giving him a generous view of the magnificent curves hiding under that dress.

The sight of her long slim legs and the sweeping curve of her breasts had thrown him off balance. A vision of himself running his hands slowly along her shapely calves, up over her knees and between her soft thighs, had hit him like a belt in the face and he'd found himself losing his legendary cool. His hands were still shaking from the effort of keeping them by his sides.

She was clearly trouble—which he should back the hell away from. He had no patience with career women who valued their jobs above everything and *everyone* else. His mother had been one, and even though he'd resented her in so many ways somehow he'd found himself in relationships with women who turned out to be just like her. But he'd learnt his lesson. Enough was enough. Despite finding himself dangerously attracted to Josie, he wouldn't allow anything to happen between them.

He watched as she stood up and stretched her arms above her head.

'Right, I'm off for a walk. See you later.'

She slipped on her flip-flops, pulled on a sunhat and stalked away from the terrace, her sundress swishing around her endless legs. The woman was a bundle of nervous energy.

She could definitely do with having some fun.

CHAPTER THREE

AFTER DOZING FITFULLY in the sun for an hour Connor went back into the kitchen to find it had been turned into a laundry. There was a piece of clothing on every chair, and the pièce de résistance was the array of underwear hung in a neat row over the oven door.

Nice.

He laughed to himself. The woman had balls.

If this was her attempt to make him uncomfortable about staying here she was in for a big disappointment. It was going to take a lot more than parading her knickers in the kitchen to get rid of him.

Lifting a bra from the rail, he rubbed the silky material between finger and thumb. It had been a long while since he'd got his hands on a woman's underwear; that had to be the reason why he was as hard as concrete again.

Dropping it back onto the rail, he hurriedly left the kitchen and went for a cooling shower—only to find her girly crap spread all over the room up there as well. The fruity smell of her shampoo still hung in the air. He shook his head in wonder; she was a feisty one. Well, two could play that game.

After a day of lying low and desperately trying to find things to entertain her that weren't work-related Josie found she was actually looking forward to having some company for supper.

She'd decided to take a short break from writing the tender document just while Connor was here—hopefully that wouldn't be for too much longer. Abi had wanted her to have a proper break, and she'd promised she wouldn't work while she was here to placate her. If Connor some-how let slip to Abi that she'd ignored her promise there would be trouble. She couldn't afford to piss her business partner off any more than she already had. Everything would fall apart if they couldn't work together any more.

As soon as eight o'clock came around she went down to the kitchen to find Connor stirring something at the stove. Her underwear was still hanging limply on the rail in front of him. As she watched he reached down and grabbed a pair of her knickers, rubbing his hands on them as if they were a tea towel. He turned when she let out an involuntary gasp and nodded to her, as if it was perfectly normal to be cleaning his hands on ladies' underwear.

Marching over, she snatched her knickers out of his hand and gathered the rest from the rail, bumping her arm into the hard muscle of his abdomen in her hurry.

'Careful, there, I might start thinking you're trying to get into my pants, what with all the groping and the exhibiting of your undercrackers,' he said.

Turning to make eye contact, she found they were so close she could smell the spicy heat of him. There was a strange throbbing in her throat, as if her pulse was trying to break free and become its own entity. Concentrating on the laughter lines at the side of his eyes, she attempted to centre herself. The sun had deepened his tan, which only made the vivid blue of his eyes stand out more.

She opened her mouth to reply but nothing came out.

'Not lost for words, Josie, surely?'

Before she had chance to pull herself together and form a suitably cutting reply he gave her another blast of that awesome smile and she melted again.

He knew exactly what she was up to; she could see the amusement in the depths of his eyes and in the jaunty angle of his eyebrow. Why the hell had she thought a pair of her knickers would scare off a man like him? What had compelled her to sink so low?

Desperation.

She was a mess. And now so were her knickers.

As all the connotations of *that* thought hit her she was totally unable to stop a full-blown grin spreading across her face. Then a giggle broke free, and then a great heaving laugh. Once she started she couldn't stop. Turning away and taking a step back, she steadied herself against the kitchen chair until she managed to get the convulsions under control.

'My God, you're a handful.' She shook her head in bewildered despair, but it felt good to laugh out loud.

He raised an eyebrow. 'I rather think I am.' He leant back against the stove. 'Maybe two handfuls.'

At this, she started giggling again, like a nervous teenager, and he joined in with a deep chuckle.

Why had it been so long since she'd laughed with someone like this?

He moved towards her and her giggle fit subsided. She was acutely aware of how his shorts and T-shirt fitted his body perfectly. How soft the golden skin of his throat looked. How much she wanted to feel the strength of him under her hands.

'I know you're trying to get rid of me, Josie, but I'm not budging. You can put up with me for a couple of days, right?'

It was more of an order than a question.

She ran through her options.

There were none.

It wasn't as if she'd be able to physically chuck him out, and he seemed totally uninterested in her perfectly reasonable points of argument.

Ah, what the hell? She could put up with him for a short while. At least it would help to break the boredom. It was kind of fun, sparring with him. He was stimulating company, and she was rather enjoying just looking at him.

'Okay. Fine. But the bed's mine.'

He held his hands up. 'You women and your passion for beds.'

'Clinophilia.'

'I'm sorry?'

'Having a passion for beds is clinophilia.'

He gave her a stunned smile. 'You just pulled that out of the air?'

She shrugged. 'It's general knowledge.'

He snorted. 'Is it?' He raised a seductive eyebrow. 'Well, far be it from me to kick a lady out of my bed.'

She shook her head in wonder at his gall. 'You can't resist a double entendre, can you, Connor?'

'I can't help myself when I'm around you, Josie.'

She was so breathless she had to concentrate hard on sucking air into her constricted lungs. The combination of flirty talk and the proximity of his to-die-for body was having a devastating effect on her.

'It's nearly time to eat,' he said quietly, a mirthful smile in his eyes.

He knew. He knew all too well.

She realised she was gawping at him and dragged her gaze away.

'Smells great,' she muttered.

When she glanced back at him the look on his face

made her insides flip over. Breaking eye contact, he turned back to the stove and added some herbs to the pan. She felt the loss of his attention keenly, as if the sun had slipped behind a cloud.

Drumming her fingers against her legs, she looked around the kitchen for something to do, her nerves jumping.

'Do you need any help? With supper?'

He looked back and gave her a lopsided grin. 'I think it's probably better if I take care of it.' He gestured towards the work surface. 'No microwave,' he said by way of explanation.

Her hackles rose. 'Just because I don't cook at home, it doesn't mean I can't be useful in the kitchen.'

He just smiled, not rising to her cross tone. 'I've got this covered—but, thanks.'

She shifted from foot to foot before leaning awkwardly against the chair-back. She was reluctant to be on her own again after spending all day bored out of her brain.

He watched her in bemusement. 'If you want something to read there are yesterday's newspapers in the snug.'

He wasn't making it easy for her to stay and watch him.

'Okay, then.' She swung her finger to point behind her. 'I'll get out of your hair for a bit.'

'Okay.' He waved his hand, as if dismissing her, turning back to the stove without another word.

Supper was a sumptuously tender boeuf bourguignon with buttery new potatoes and crispy green beans. Josie wolfed it down with barely a pause. Neither of them spoke during the meal except to exchange pleasantries, which suited her fine.

She wasn't sure why she felt so nervous around him.

She'd faced CEOs of multi-million-pound corporations and been less jittery than this. He had some kind of strange effect on her, and she found it distressing. She should be able to handle this, no problem, but just his presence next to her set her mind into a spin. Every movement he made sent vibrations along her nerves. His gestures were precise, but elegant, and she thought she could probably watch him for hours and not grow bored.

'That was delicious, thanks,' she said, leaning back in her chair.

'You're welcome. Woman should not live on corn-flakes alone,' he said, giving her a look of reproach.

She grinned sheepishly, then tapped her hands gently on the table, beating out a rhythm.

Connor continued to watch her as she battled with the unwelcome warmth spreading through her under his intense gaze.

The silence between them lengthened.

'So, how do you usually spend your evenings?' she asked, trying to break the atmosphere.

Connor's brow furrowed as he gave it some thought. 'Game of chess?'

'Chess, huh? Okay. I've not played in a while, but what the hell?'

'I warn you, I take no prisoners.' He wagged a finger at her.

'Thanks for the warning,' she said, going into the snug and grabbing the chessboard.

Neither did she.

'Ah, the Corporate Opening,' Connor joked as Josie moved her first piece.

'Always works for me,' she said, looking up at him through her eyelashes.

Connor didn't hesitate before moving his first piece.

'Hmm, the Nomad Defence. Daring,' Josie said, an eyebrow raised in jest.

'They don't call me Crazy-eyed Connor for nothing.'

'Do they really?'

'Actually, no.' He pretended to look sad.

'So, how else do you entertain yourself when you're travelling?' She tapped her fingers against her leg whilst studying the board for her next move. She was determined to win this game.

'When I get the chance I go mountaineering—sometimes ice climbing.'

Josie raised both eyebrows this time. 'Action man, huh?'

'Got to get my kicks somehow.'

'Right.' She moved another piece, holding on to it for a few seconds before releasing it.

'You, I see, have a more cautious nature.'

She shrugged. 'I don't like making mistakes.'

Connor laughed. 'Some of my worst mistakes have led to the most interesting times I've ever had.'

'I'll take your word for it.'

'You've never been tempted by extreme sports?' He looked up at her before glancing down to move his next piece.

'Not unless you count falling out of a tree.'

He smiled. 'Ah, so there *is* an adventurous spirit in there somewhere, then?'

'No, not really, but a friend dared me.'

Connor smiled again. 'And you never back down, right?'

Josie looked at him steadily. 'Something like that,' she said, moving another piece.

Twenty minutes later Connor was scratching his head in bewilderment. 'You're good.'

'What's with the surprise?'

He barked out a laugh. 'I don't get beaten very often.'

He held her gaze for a moment; he was looking for something, but she wasn't sure what. His pupils dilated as he gazed at her and once again a strange swooping feeling hit her deep inside. Her skin tingled and the breath hitched in her throat. They were two feet apart, but she felt the connection as if she was caught in a tractor beam.

How did he *do* that?

Not sure how to handle the feeling, she broke her gaze and sat back in the chair, trying to get some distance between them, her fingers dancing at her sides.

Connor was disappointed when Josie looked away. He was trying to figure out if she was for real. He'd been burned before by women trying to worm their way into his affections and he was suspicious about the apparent softening in her attitude. Perhaps this was another ruse to try and get rid of him somehow. He needed to be careful.

On the outside she seemed genuine enough. Despite her spikiness, or maybe because of it, he wanted her, and now she was showing a softer side he wanted her even more. This was driving him crazy. But he'd be a fool to get involved with her right now. He should do himself a favour and put some distance between them before it was too late.

Picking up a newspaper to look at the crossword, he found Josie had already completed it.

'What the...? When did you do this?' He smacked his hand against the paper.

Josie looked across at him. 'Hmm? When you were cooking dinner. Sorry, did you want to finish it? I thought maybe you were stuck.' There was a glimmer of mischief in her eyes.

He scowled. 'I did, but I'd just had a brainwave.' He

peered at the crossword. 'Although apparently I hadn't.'
He shook his head, perplexed. He picked up the other
paper only to find she'd finished the crossword in that
too. These were tough cryptic puzzles that he'd been
struggling with for hours.

'Did you do these in that fifteen minutes before dinner?'

'Yeah.' She flushed under his scrutiny.

'Do you have some crazily high IQ or something?'

She shuffled in her seat, drawing her knees up onto
the sofa, her body forming a fetal position. 'I don't know.
I've never been tested.'

'Really?'

She shrugged. 'I'm good at remembering things. I
don't always understand them—not like...' She paused,
looking down at her hands. An evasive manoeuvre.

'Not like...?' He wanted to push this; there was obviously more to it than she was letting on.

'Not like some people.'

'It sounded like you had someone in mind there.'

'Hmm...'

He could tell by the way her eyes shifted sharply to
the left that she was hoping to escape the subject by acting dumb. Not a hope in hell.

'Who are you talking about, Josie?'

She sighed, the weight of her reluctance heavy in her
breath. 'My sister Maddie. Madeline Marchpane.' She
gave him a look, as if she was waiting for him to connect the dots, for the correct synapses to snap together.

Then the penny dropped.

Madeline Marchpane was in the media a lot, cele-
brated for being a sexy genius scientist. She had a popular show in which she explained complex theories in

layman's terms. The public had lapped her up. That was
why Josie's name and face had dinged those bells for him.

'Are you twins?'

'She's two years older than me.'

'You look a lot alike.'

'I know.'

He smiled. 'And she *has* had her IQ tested?'

Josie snorted gently. There was a world of pain in that
short exhalation of breath. 'Yes.'

'That must be a tough gig to compete with.'

'I wish I could say I got the beauty and she got the
brains, but it wouldn't be true.' It was obviously a line
she wheeled out on a regular basis, and her attempt at
flippancy was totally unconvincing.

'You think you're second best to your sister?'

She frowned. 'We can't all be exceptional.'

'You think you're not exceptional?'

She laughed—a low, tense chuckle. 'I do okay.'

'Jeez, no wonder you're so strung out.'

Her gaze snapped to his. 'You think I'm strung out
because I have a successful sister?' She leant forward in
her chair, a deep scowl marring her beautiful face. 'I'm
stressed because my business is in jeopardy and I've been
ordered to go on bloody *holiday.*'

The sudden flash of anger surprised him, but it left
her face as quickly as it had come. There was that look
again: the swiftly shifting gaze, the tensing of her jawline, the flicker of a frown. As if she was internally rep-
rimanding herself for something. She'd done it the last
time her tone had slipped into aggressiveness.

'Who *ordered* you?'

'Your sister.'

'Why would she do that? And why the hell would you
listen to her?'

There was a tense pause before she spoke again. 'Because of a thing at work.'

'A *thing*?'

She rubbed a hand over her eyes, then batted away his question. 'I've been working fifteen-hour days for weeks and I'm exhausted. Abi thinks I need to step away from work for a while.'

Her whole posture had slouched, as if she'd drawn right into herself.

'So she sent you here to do cold turkey?'

She didn't look up. 'I agreed to come here for a break.'

'It's a good job your laptop's bust and you haven't been writing tenders, then,' he said wryly.

A muscle ticked in her jaw.

'You okay, Josie?'

She looked up sharply. 'I'm fine. Just tired. In fact, I think I'll go to bed.' She unfurled herself and stood up. 'Goodnight.'

She didn't look back as she left the room.

Interesting.

The next morning Josie came downstairs to find the sun pouring in through the patio doors in the kitchen, bathing everything in golden light. There was no sign of Connor and the door to the snug was firmly shut. The heavy tension that had built since she'd woken dropped down a notch.

She'd felt spun out last night, after their conversation about Maddie and work, and had tossed and turned for an hour before falling into a fitful sleep. He'd hit on some real bruises this time, and she didn't like it one bit. She was going to have to be more careful about what she said around him from this point onwards. He was too perceptive for his own good and she'd already told him more than she was comfortable with.

Only a couple more days, Josie, then he'll be gone.

Pushing him to the back of her mind, she moved about almost in a dream, making coffee and heaping cereal into a bowl. Even in the sunny calm of the kitchen she felt weirdly buzzed, as if she was anticipating something momentous but had no idea what.

Just as she was pouring herself another coffee Connor strode in, bare-chested, his hair rumpled with sleep, his eyes tired.

'Morning,' she said, turning to hide the blush that crept up her neck at the sight of him. Her heart slammed uncomfortably against her chest and she took a long, slow breath in an attempt to calm down.

'Morning,' he mumbled. 'How was my bed?'

She forced herself to look at him, determined not to give away how flustered she was. 'Very comfortable. How was the sofa?'

He grimaced and rubbed the back of his neck. 'Short and lumpy.'

Stifling her smile, Josie grabbed another mug, poured in the remainder of the coffee and handed it to him.

'Thanks.' He took a long sip, wincing as he swallowed. 'You like your coffee strong.'

She only just stopped herself saying *Like my men.* Where the heck had this one-track mind sprung from?

They ate breakfast together in silence, the tense atmosphere from the night before still hanging between them.

'So, what are your plans for the day?' he said finally.

She shrugged. 'I don't have any. A bit of reading, maybe. A short walk. Some relaxing…' She noticed a smile playing around his lips. 'What?'

'I can't imagine you sitting around relaxing, that's all.

You're the least relaxed person I've ever met. You always look as if you're itching to move on to the next thing.'

'Yeah, well, I'm not used to sitting still.'

'You're a nervous breakdown waiting to happen. You know that?'

She gave him a tight smile, fighting down her irritation that he seemed to be picking up right where they'd left off last night. 'I haven't got time for a breakdown. My schedule wouldn't allow it.'

He gave her a mirthful stare. 'You plan everything?'

She straightened the skirt of her halter-neck dress. 'I like to know what I'm doing.'

'I'm surprised you haven't got more of a plan for the day, then—or are you freestyling for the challenge?'

Josie tipped her head thoughtfully. She hadn't got beyond thinking about what she was going to have for breakfast, taking the day one step at a time. But if she couldn't work she was going to have to think of something pretty soon, before she died of boredom.

'Something like that.' She swept her hand around the stillness of the kitchen and the unbroken landscape that stretched away from them outside. 'There's not a whole lot going on around here, so I'm going to have to make my own fun.'

He looked at her then and their gazes locked. His pupils darkened, turning his eyes black. He held her gaze, drawing her into a world of fiery longing. What the hell was going on? A need to touch him almost overwhelmed her. Her stomach did a double flip and her fingers itched to run over his golden skin, tracing the swell of muscles over his arms, across his shoulders, down his chest...

Bad idea.

It had been such a long time since she'd been so attracted to someone it had thrown her into chaos. She'd forgotten how exciting it was, how much fun. Not that this could be any more than a passing whim. She should enjoy the novelty of it but give herself boundaries. Stay in control.

'Uh...do you fancy another game of chess?' she asked, pulling her thoughts back onto safe ground before she started drooling. It had been entertaining playing last night, especially when he'd been so disgusted when she'd beaten him.

He shook his head. 'I can't. I'm meeting a friend for lunch in Aix.'

'Oh, okay.' She kept her tone light, but was annoyed by how disappointed she felt.

'You could always walk up to Guy's farm and get some eggs. They're great when they're really fresh. Just head north-east. It's a couple of miles away across the fields.' He waved in the direction he meant. 'It shouldn't take you more than half an hour to get there.'

'Yeah, okay. I might do that.' Her wayward voice had taken on a childishly reluctant tone without her consent.

Connor didn't appear to notice. 'Want me to draw you a map?'

She shoved her shoulders back in defiance at his cod-dling behaviour—before remembering his comment about her 'magnificent rack' and adjusting her posture to make her stance less overtly aggressive. 'No, thanks. I'm sure I can find it,' she said coolly.

'Don't leave it too late to walk over there. The heat gets pretty fierce after midday.' His face was blank of emotion but she was pretty sure he was deliberately wind-ing her up again.

'Okay,' she said, gripping her mug hard.

She wasn't sure why she was so cross with him. She almost felt as if he was abandoning her by going out, which was patently ridiculous. She was a grown-up who was perfectly capable of entertaining herself.

Wasn't she?

The truth was she never had to do it at home, because she was either thinking about or totally engrossed in work. Being away from it left a big gap in her psyche.

'Okay. Well, I'm making omelettes tonight, so we're definitely going to need eggs from somewhere.'

She put her mug down carefully on the table before she threw it at his smug head. 'You don't have to feed me, you know.' Her teeth were beginning to hurt from being clamped together so hard.

'It's just as easy to make food for two people,' he said, shrugging. 'What are you going to have if you don't eat with me?'

That was a good point. There wasn't exactly a lot of food in the house, and the meal he'd made last night had been delicious. She should consider it his fee for her agreeing to share the place; he wasn't exactly the easiest housemate to live with and she should get some sort of recompense for it.

'Want me to pick some up in town instead?' he asked, obviously irked at her slow response.

'No. It's fine. I'll go to the farm,' she said through tight lips.

'Great.' He smiled and went to slap her on the arm, but stopped himself. Their gazes snagged and he gave her a curt nod. 'Make sure you lock up properly when you go out. See you later.'

He turned and walked out, pulling the door shut a little too hard behind him so that it slammed against the frame.

After taking a rather circuitous route to the farm a couple of hours later, Josie finally arrived hot and frustrated.

The farmyard was deserted, so she knocked on the heavy oak door to the house. It was heaved open a few seconds later by a short, burly man with a thatch of wiry black hair.

'*Oui?*'

'Hello, Guy, I'm staying with Connor Preston in the farmhouse over there,' Josie said in French. 'I would like to buy some eggs from you.'

The man gave her a slow up-and-down inspection.

'*Oui.*'

His gaze lingered on her breasts and she had to work hard not to cross her arms defensively in front of her.

Great—a pervy farmer. Just what she needed.

'Come to the runs with me. I need to collect them,' he said, gesturing to the side of the house, where a collection of ramshackle barns and pens stood.

She followed Guy at a distance and watched as he checked the nests for newly laid eggs.

Walking back to her with a smile, he stood a little bit too close for comfort as he carefully put the eggs into the bag she'd brought with her. He smelt of dirt and cigarettes and *wrongness*. Wrinkling her nose, she forced herself to stand still. She often found herself turned off people because they didn't smell right, and he was definitely one of those people.

'Thanks.' She took a polite step away from him and handed over a five-euro note.

'You want some change?' he said, making it sound more as if he was asking her if she wanted a good seeing-to.

Her skin crawled at the thought.

'No. Keep it,' she said, backing away further and holding up a placatory hand.

'How about a drink before you go?' he asked.

She was feeling really uncomfortable now. It wasn't as if she'd never been indirectly propositioned, but she was acutely aware of how alone she was here. He was probably just being friendly, she told herself, but she didn't want to hang around and find out. Her heart was firing like a piston in her chest and she felt dizzy and disorientated in the heat.

'No, thank you. I have to get back. Connor's waiting for me.' Nerves made her tone snippy.

Guy looked affronted by her rejection of his hospitality, but shrugged and turned and walked away, leaving her there feeling like the rudest woman on earth. Her people skills clearly needed some work.

Not that she didn't already know that. Abi had made it abundantly clear that she was becoming increasingly difficult to work with. The heavy sinking feeling she'd been dodging for the past couple of days landed squarely on her shoulders. She shook it off. It would all be fine once she got back to London. She'd make sure it was.

She started walking back the way she'd come. The trouble with this place was it looked the same for miles around. There was a tree she thought she recognised in the distance so she made her way towards it, pulling off the heads of some lavender as she went and pinching them between her fingers to release the scent. Lavender was supposed to be good for helping you relax wasn't it? She was going to need a tonne of it at this rate.

After an hour of stomping through the fields she began to regret not taking better notice of which way she'd come. She still hadn't found the farmhouse and she was baking in the fierce heat of the sun.

There was very little shade—just the odd small olive tree dotted here and there. Her mouth felt uncomfortably dry, and the more she thought about it the thirstier she got.

She couldn't remember the last time she'd experienced such intense heat. Her last holiday had been a skiing trip three years ago, which she'd had to cut short because of a crisis at work. Her job had taken her abroad a couple of times, but she'd always been ferried from air-conditioned plane to air-conditioned office. There had never been time for any sightseeing, so she'd just been left with the impression of heat and humidity as an abstract concept.

In short, she was well out of her depth.

Connor knew there was something wrong as soon as he pulled up to the front of the farmhouse. The heavy oak door was ajar and when he cautiously pushed it open he was greeted by the sure signs of a robbery. All the drawers of the hall sideboard were lying tipped upside down on the floor, surrounded by their contents. It was the same story in the kitchen. The digital radio and a couple of his grandmother's old ornaments were missing from the snug, but they hadn't bothered with the ancient TV.

He stood listening for a few seconds, his heart racing from a mixture of anger and fear in case they were still in the house, but it was silent. Luckily there wasn't anything much of value they could have taken, but he was furious about the violation of his property and the mess they'd made.

Taking the stairs two at a time, he checked each of the bedrooms. They'd had a go at opening a couple of his boxes of books and climbing equipment, but had obviously abandoned them as not worth the time. In Josie's room the drawers spewed her underwear and linen. The only thing he couldn't see was her laptop. Maybe she'd taken it to be repaired? No, she couldn't have done. Her car was still in the driveway.

Where *was* she?

A thread of fear twisted through him. Surely she'd been out when they'd broken in. Maybe she'd gone to the farm as he'd suggested? He really hoped so.

After making a sweep of the garden and the garage, and thankfully not finding her trussed up with her head bashed in, he went to phone Guy at the farm to see if she'd turned up there. Blood thumped through his veins as he waited for him to pick up.

'Allo?'

'Guy, it's Connor Preston.'

'Bonjour, Connor. *Ça va?'*

'I'm great, thanks, Guy. Listen, did a woman come and buy some eggs from you?'

There was a pause. *'Oui.* She left about an hour ago. I offered her a drink, because she didn't have one with her, but she wasn't interested in being friendly.'

Connor let out a long, low breath, finally allowing himself to relax. That sounded exactly like Josie. Guy was clearly unimpressed by her naivety. 'An hour ago, did you say?'

'Oui.'

'Okay. Thanks, Guy.'

'No problem.'

Connor replaced the handset and stood there thinking. She couldn't have been here for the robbery, then, but if she'd left the farm an hour ago she should be back by now.

The sun was beating down relentlessly and he knew she'd be having trouble finding shade out there. The flat French landscape didn't provide such a luxury. If she hadn't had a drink for a while she'd be pretty dehydrated.

He ran his hands through his hair in agitation. The

last thing he needed right now was to have to babysit some stupid townie with no sense of survival. She was stubborn and self-involved, and would no doubt be angry with him for chasing after her, but he knew he couldn't leave her out there in this heat. He'd deal with the break-in once he knew she was safe.

After grabbing a bottle of water from the kitchen, he strode off in the direction of the farm.

Josie was drenched in sweat. Her dress stuck to her legs and her hair fell in clumps around her face.

A while back she'd slowed down to look about her, and had realised she could no longer recognise any land-marks. Lavender fields stretched out on all sides of her, each direction seemingly identical to the others. Panic lay heavy in her stomach as she realised she was lost. Logi-cally, she should be able to retrace her steps, but the heat was making her head fuzzy, and she'd taken a few turns without marking them in her mind, and now she wasn't sure if she could remember them.

She turned back, but wasn't sure she was heading in the right direction.

Oh, God…oh, God.

Blood pounded through her veins as her body strug-gled to keep cool in the relentless heat. Her skin was boiling to the touch and her head thumped under the bright glare of the sun. She was exhausted. Her muscles screamed at her to stop and rest, but she was too pan-icked. She needed to keep going.

What she wouldn't give for a drink of water right now. Or just a bit of shade.

What had she been thinking? How could she have been so stupid? She'd been so desperate to show Connor she didn't need his help with a map she'd put herself in danger.

Struggling on slowly, she fanned her hands in front of her face in a vain attempt to cool herself down. There wasn't a breath of wind in the air. It was like walking through soup.

Her foot hit a bit of uneven ground and her legs went from under her. She lay there, sprawled out on the dry earth, willing her body to move, but it refused. The blood pounding in her ears was keeping time with the sharp ache in her head.

Boom, boom-boom, boom.

All she could do was concentrate on the sound; it was taking over everything else.

She didn't know how long she'd been lying there when she became aware of a gentle vibration in the ground and a shadow fell across her. Forcing her aching head to turn and look at its source was agonising. All she could make out was a large silhouette blocking out the sun.

'Josie, are you okay?' Connor's voice sounded urgent.

Her mouth wouldn't form the words she needed; it was so dry her tongue stuck to the roof of her mouth. She managed to shake her head, sending off a fresh wave of pain, forcing her to close her eyes against it. She was vaguely aware of Connor putting a bottle to her lips and liquid pouring into her parched mouth. She could barely swallow, but he kept it there until he was satisfied she'd taken some down. She felt him wrap something wet around her head and shoulders before lifting her up into his arms.

Laying her head against his bare chest, she closed her eyes and relaxed into the gentle rocking motion of his body as he set off walking. She could feel the muscles moving under his skin as he held her to him. She snuggled tighter, like a cat rubbing in for a stroke.

'What were you *thinking*?'

His voice rumbled in his chest next to her right ear. He sounded more worried than angry, which surprised her. She could smell a mixture of suntan lotion and the musk of his skin and inhaled deeply, glad of the distraction from her pounding head. Despite the pain, she felt almost euphoric. She took little sips from the bottle he'd given her, relishing the coldness of the water as it slipped down her throat.

Josie had no idea how long it took them to get back to the farmhouse. Her thoughts swam in and out of focus as she fought the desire to fall asleep; it was so peaceful here in his arms that she didn't want to miss a minute of it.

CHAPTER FOUR

THE NEXT THING she was aware of was the cool darkness of the farmhouse as Connor stepped in through the door. Getting out of the bright glare of the sun was a huge relief, and her spirits soared as the reassuring sounds and smells of the place filled her senses.

He carried her straight upstairs and put her carefully down on the bed. Being hugged against his hard body had been so comforting; she couldn't remember when she'd last been held so close for so long and she missed his touch as soon as he released her from his arms.

Lying back on the cool sheets, she opened her eyes to see Connor standing over her, his body gleaming with sweat. Before she could utter a word he removed his damp shirt from around her head, then moved down her body to slip off her shoes.

'What are you doing?' Her voice sounded strangely languorous to her ears and he stopped what he was doing and looked at her, his gaze raking her face. For one mad moment she thought he was going to bend down and kiss her. Her insides burned hot with anticipation.

'We need to get you in a cool bath.'

To her disappointment his voice was brisk and professional. Her heart sank. He wasn't going to kiss her. Not that that would have been in any way appropriate, she reminded herself sternly.

'We have to get your body temperature down. You've got heat exhaustion.'

Josie bit her lip and nodded her agreement. Heat exhaustion. He must think she was such an idiot. 'Okay.'

Connor helped her slowly ease the soaked sundress over her body. She lifted her pelvis off the bed, then her shoulders, so it could be pulled up and over her head. She watched his face the whole time, her heart thudding erratically in her chest. He seemed to be concentrating hard on his task, but she noticed his gaze flitting up and down her body, resting for a second on her breasts, which were barely concealed by the thin lace of her bra.

Thank God she'd put her decent underwear on that morning.

There was a pause, as if he was going to say something, and they both hung there, suspended in the moment. Heat flooded between her legs and instinctively she arched her back towards him, pushing her breasts higher, a burning need for his touch overtaking all rational thought.

Connor tore his eyes away from her body and ran his hands roughly through his hair. 'I'll run you a bath.' Turning away from her, he flung the dress onto the chair at the far side of the room and strode out, leaving her lying there with her cheeks burning.

She heard the sound of running water in the bathroom and rocked her head back on the pillow, pinching her eyes shut. She felt like such a fool. What must he think of her? She was acting like a wanton hussy after he'd been forced to come out and rescue her.

Was it possible to sink any lower?

Connor returned a minute later and gestured for her

to open her mouth, so he could put a thermometer under her tongue. Kneeling down beside the bed, he took her pulse, his fingers cool against the hot skin of her wrist.

She forced herself to turn and watch him, fighting down the sting of her humiliation. His gaze was fixed on his watch, his jaw tense, as he counted the beats of her heart. With a sinking feeling she acknowledged that *she* was responsible for that deep crease of concern on his forehead—and for the look of exhaustion in his eyes. The realisation that his quick thinking and superior knowledge had probably saved her life hit her like a punch to the solar plexus.

'How do you know how to do all this?' she asked, her voice wobbly with humility.

He looked up in surprise. 'I've had first aid training. It's important to know what to do in an emergency when the nearest hospital is a hundred miles away.'

'Yes, of course, that makes sense.' Perhaps she'd underestimated him when it came to his travelling. This cool efficiency was a whole side to him she hadn't even glimpsed before.

'Okay, time for your bath. Want me to carry you? Or can you walk?'

He was looking at her so intently a small shiver ran down her spine.

He's only looking at you like that because he's worried he's in the company of a lunatic. Pull yourself together.

'I can walk,' she said, desperate now to appear more confident than she felt, even though she wasn't sure she had the strength even to get up. Willing her body to function, she sat up unsteadily, then managed to roll off the bed and onto her feet. There was no way she'd ask him to carry her again. She still had some vestige of pride.

Her legs were like jelly. Moving slowly to the bathroom, she imagined she could feel Connor's gaze burning into her back and she willed him to leave her to lick her wounds in mortified isolation. It was so undignified, shuffling across the floor in just her underwear, but she kept her head high and didn't look back.

She didn't realise he'd followed her until she turned to close the bathroom door.

'I said I'm okay.' This came out more harshly than she'd intended, and she gripped the door handle hard in frustration, feeling the metal bite into her hand. Taking a steadying breath, she smiled, trying to soften the effect of her response, but Connor just shrugged.

'I wanted to make sure you didn't get dizzy and bash your head,' he said, obviously battling to keep the wry expression off his face and failing spectacularly.

She would never live this down. Never. She knew it. He was going to remind her of her stupidity at every opportunity he could find before he moved on. 'Well, as you can see, I made it okay,' she said, her tone snappy and defensive.

'Why are you so cross with me?' He seemed genuinely surprised by her anger.

She wasn't being fair, punishing him for things he hadn't even done yet. Sighing, she rubbed a hand over her eyes and sat on the edge of the bath before her legs gave way. 'I'm angry with myself for being such an idiot. I can't believe you had to come out and rescue me. It's pathetic.' She looked at him directly and frowned at his reaction. 'Why are you smiling?'

'Because I knew you'd act like this. You don't strike me as the sort of person who'd tolerate being a damsel in distress.'

Her shoulders slumped. 'Let's put it down to a lapse in judgement. I don't know what's got into me lately.'

'Those mistakes just keep happening, huh?'

'Yeah.' She took a deep breath, blinking back tears that had come out of nowhere.

He frowned and took a step backwards. 'Right, well, I'll go and make up a salt solution for you to drink while you're in there. You need to replace your fluids.'

Turning briskly, he marched out, leaving her staring after him.

Connor took the stairs two at a time in an effort to get away from Josie as fast as he could.

His hands shook as he measured out the salt and water for her rehydration drink—half a teaspoon to one litre of water, and a dash of orange to disguise the taste.

The vision of her in just her underwear was still emblazoned on his eyes and no matter where he looked there the image was.

The sight of her breasts practically spilling out of that see-through bra had nearly sent him over the edge. He'd wanted to touch her. To release her from the restricting cups, slide down that scrap of lace that passed for her knickers and leave her totally exposed to his hungry gaze.

Under the circumstances, he knew how inappropriate his reaction had been, but he hadn't been able to help himself. He was a red-blooded male who hadn't been near a woman for the past nine months. Surely it was to be expected?

He sighed, low and long, exhausted from the walk back with Josie in his arms and the monumental battle to keep his libido under control. He was desperate for a nap, but he knew he needed to get fluids into her before she slept. Dehydration was a dangerous beast.

It had been a shock to find her in such a state. When he'd first seen her for one awful minute he'd thought he was too late. She'd been lying in a heap, as if passed out, her sundress splayed around her, a splash of white in the surrounding lavender fields. The relief at finding her still conscious had been acute, and the adrenaline rush had stayed with him for most of the walk back.

Just now, when her face had fallen and she'd looked close to tears, he'd had to make a sharp exit. If he'd moved towards her instead of out through the door who knew what would have happened?

Tossing the spoon into the sink, he took another couple of seconds to compose himself. He was so unused to actively battling his reactions it had him freaked, and he didn't want Josie picking up on it. They were already walking a very fine line between friendly acquaintance and something dangerously intense. Just one tiny push from her would have him in free fall, and this was not the time for him to lose his fragile grip on control.

He carried the glass of liquid carefully upstairs and knocked on the bathroom door. He didn't wait for her response and walked straight in, keeping his eyes down to protect her modesty as well as his state of mind.

'Don't worry, I'm not staying.'

'I'm not worried,' she said, her voice strained.

He felt her take the glass from his outstretched hand and turned back towards the door. He was twitchy, and desperate to get out of there, but he wanted to check she was over the worst.

'So how are you feeling now? Any dizziness? Irregular breathing?' He heard the swish and splash of water as she stood and stepped out of the bath.

'No,' she said.

Her voice was softer than before. Was that shame he could sense in her tone? He felt suddenly protective of her. She must have been terrified out there on her own.

People misjudged the danger of being out in the heat all the time, thinking they were okay right up until it was too late.

'Good. It sounds like you're recovering okay. You'll need to rest up and sleep it off. You've put your body through quite an ordeal.'

There was a pause.

'Connor?'

'Yeah?' He turned round to face her. She'd wrapped a thick towelling robe around herself and it swamped her slender frame. She looked younger and oddly vulnerable. An uncomfortable pressure squeezed his abdomen and there was a strange buzzing in his head.

'Thank you.'

He shook his head, trying to clear it. 'It's okay, really. It could have happened to anyone.' He smiled, hoping to lighten the atmosphere.

'I'm not thinking straight at the moment.'

'Because of the *thing* at work?'

He didn't know what had made him ask that right then, but he found he really wanted to hear the answer. All this over-reactive behaviour had to be linked to something. She was clearly a clever woman who was having a hard time dealing with whatever had brought her here to the farmhouse.

She laughed quietly. 'You're determined to get a straight answer out of me, aren't you?'

He shrugged. 'I'm a nosy bastard.'

She sat carefully on the edge of the bath and stared down at the floor, her hair falling across her face. 'It's a tough marketplace and we're fighting every day to keep and win new business.' Her voice was steady, but emotionless. 'There aren't a lot of contracts up for grabs in this climate. It's harsh out there. Eat or be eaten.'

An image of his sister as a young, determined girl flashed into his mind. He could see why she'd chosen Josie as a business partner. He crossed his arms and looked out of the window, trying to eradicate the feeling of unease this train of thought triggered.

'You don't really want to hear all this crap,' Josie said, breaking into his thoughts.

'It's okay.' He shrugged. 'I've been told I'm a good listener.' He refused to give any more brain space to his sister. That particular direction in the maze of his life was a dead end now.

'You are.'

She was smiling at him when he looked back.

'But I need to sleep and I should let you have a shower.'

'I smell that bad, huh?' He raised an eyebrow, hoping humour would drag him out of his funk.

'Of course not…that's not what I meant.' Her cheeks were adorably flushed.

He flapped a hand at her to show he was only joking. 'Okay, get some rest.' He backed towards the door. 'Bang on the floor if you want anything, okay?'

'Okay,' she said as he turned and walked out into the safety of the hallway. 'Thanks for looking after me, Connor.'

The words rang out in the air behind him.

It was six o'clock in the evening before Josie woke up. Rolling onto her side, she sat up tentatively and waited for her headache to catch up with the movement. It appeared to be much reduced.

Thank God for that.

She could hear Connor banging about in the kitchen below and a delicious smell wafted up the stairs, making her stomach rumble with hunger.

Dressing quickly, she pulled a brush through her hair and checked her appearance in the mirror. She looked tired and beaten. So much for this holiday doing her some good.

The room was much more of a mess than she remembered leaving it. All the drawers of the vanity were open and clothes spilled out of them. How embarrassing. Connor must think she was a real slovenly slut. She pushed the clothes back in and tidied up a bit. Looking around, she realised her laptop was no longer sitting on the window ledge. Strange. Perhaps Connor had moved it for some reason? Worry pinched at her chest and she rubbed her hand across her ribs to try and relieve it.

After taking three slow breaths, in and out, she straightened her spine and tipped up her chin. Better.

Okay, time to face the music.

She went downstairs and found him washing up at the sink.

'That's what I like to see—a man hard at work,' she joked, hoping to start things off on a light note after the edginess of their last interaction.

He turned and gave her a comical reproving look.

Good, at least she wasn't in the doghouse. 'Can I do anything to help?' she asked, trying hard not to stare at the fluid way he moved his muscular body around the kitchen. How could someone so big be that graceful?

'No. Thanks. The omelettes are ready. I'll serve them up now you're here.'

She sat at the table, her body humming with a confusing mixture of anxiety and something akin to excitement, and watched him load the plates with food, nodding her thanks as he slid one in front of her.

'Did you move my laptop?' she asked as they tucked into the food.

He took his time looking at her and she wondered why he suddenly seemed so uncomfortable. A slow sinking feeling heated her stomach.

'What is it?'

He put his cutlery down. 'We had a break-in while we were out. They took your laptop.'

She gawped at him, her befuddled brain taking a few seconds to catch up with his words. *'What?'*

'Someone jimmied the lock on the front door and got in. There wasn't a lot to steal, but your laptop was one of the things that went. I've already spoken to the police and they've given me an incident number for an insurance claim. You should check nothing else of yours has gone.'

She put her own cutlery down and dropped her head into her hands. This day just got better and better.

'But we're so remote out here. Why would they target this place?' she said, looking back up at him.

'It happens quite a bit. There are lots of holiday homes in this region. They're easy pickings.'

'Maybe someone's trying to tell me something,' she said, sighing. That was it, then. All her work on the tender document was gone.

'Maybe someone wants you to have a *real* holiday?' he said, picking up his fork again and shovelling omelette into his mouth.

'Yeah…' She felt defeated.

'You've got insurance for it, right?'

She nodded and picked at her food, suddenly not hungry any more.

He frowned at her. 'At least you weren't here when they broke in.'

'True.'

They sat in silence while Connor cleared his plate.

'Not hungry?' he asked, nodding at her food.

'No. Sorry.'

He shrugged. 'No problem. How are you feeling generally?'

'My head's still a bit painful, but nothing like it was.' She wanted to go back to bed, so the day would be over, but she didn't want to be rude to Connor. Especially after what he'd done for her. 'It's a good job you're so well trained in first aid.'

He smiled and pushed his empty plate away from him, looking out of the window. He was closing down the conversation again, but in this case she really didn't mind. She guessed it was his way of telling her to move on without dragging her through the humiliation of directly saying it. It was a kind and decent thing to do and she felt new warmth towards him.

'So what is it you'll be doing in India?' she asked, taking his hint and opening up a new conversation.

'I help set up clean water projects in the developing world. This next trip is about making contact and scoping out where the water refineries are needed most,' he said.

She looked up sharply. 'Abi never mentioned you were doing that.'

'She probably doesn't know. I've never talked to her about it.'

An unnerving heat made its way up from deep in her pelvis. He was a world champion at dropping conversational bombshells. 'She's under the impression you're swanning around the world on one long, extended holiday.'

He shrugged, but didn't say anything.

'Why didn't you tell me before? There have been plenty of opportunities. You let me think you were some kind of entitled layabout.'

He leant in conspiratorially. 'I thought you might be here spying on me and reporting back to my sister.'

Even though she knew he meant it as a joke, she was sure there was an underlying truth there.

'She misses you, you know.'

His shoulders stiffened and he broke eye contact. 'I wouldn't know. We communicate through lawyers.'

A heavy weight of sadness settled in her belly. How incredibly sad for them both. And she thought *she* had a difficult relationship with her family. At least they all spoke to each other, even if she kept her contact with them to a minimum.

'I can't imagine being that far removed from my family,' she said, leaning in to him and putting a hand on the table between them in an awkward attempt at empathy.

'We have nothing to say to one another,' he said, scowling at his empty plate.

'I think Abi would disagree.' The memory of the pain in Abi's eyes when she'd talked about him resurfaced, and something clicked together in her head.

'Let's change the subject.'

There was a finality to his tone she didn't dare challenge. Another subject it was, then. For now. She'd find a way to get through to him eventually. It was the least she could do for Abi after the trouble she'd caused.

She leant back in her chair, feigning nonchalance in an attempt to take the atmosphere down a notch or two. 'So, tell me more about your involvement in the projects. You find locations and fund them? Run them all single-handedly?'

He snorted and looked up at her with humour in his eyes, the deep scowl gone from his face. 'I have a lot of help with the day-to-day running. I research the areas that most need support, raise the capital and get the projects underway.'

'Very worthy.'

He raised a disdainful eyebrow. 'I do it because it needs doing.'

'Yes, of course, but you must get some sense of personal satisfaction out of it?'

He shrugged. 'More than I would working for a corporation obsessed with profits.'

Pushing down a niggle of annoyance, Josie said nothing to that. She wasn't sure whether he was having a dig at her job again, but he was starting to open up about himself and she didn't want to stop the flow of information by making a scene.

'I need to feel useful,' he said, turning his head to look out of the window again, so she could no longer see the expression on his face.

She paused, pondering the subtext of his words. 'Sounds like we have more in common than we realised.' She looked down at her hands, which were twisted together in her lap, the veins raised against the tight skin. She unwound them, flexing her stiff fingers.

He turned back to her and smiled. 'Yeah?'

Connor sensed that Josie wanted to say more, but was having trouble getting the words out. He knew she hadn't told him the whole story when he'd asked her about the *thing* at work; he felt it in his bones. He was going to have to force it out of her.

'What are you hiding from me, Josie?'

She sighed and there was a beat of silence as she stared at the floor, apparently trying to make a decision—perhaps about whether to finally start trusting him. He couldn't blame her; he hadn't exactly made it easy for her up till this point.

'Some of our employees have made a formal complaint against me. Apparently I made one of them so miserable she's taken long-term sick leave, citing depression.'

She looked up at him with agony in her eyes and his stomach lurched uncomfortably. That was the last thing he'd expected her to say, and for the first time in his life he was at a loss for how to respond.

'Ah...'

'Yeah. Not my proudest moment.'

'So you're the Boss from Hell?' He tried keeping his tone light, to show he was joking, but her face dropped even more.

'I know I ask a lot of them, and I'm not the type of boss to be all chummy with my team, but we can't afford to make mistakes. Not ones that cost the business money or spoil our reputation. I guess I'm not good at communicating that without sounding like I'm having a go. People skills are not my strong point, as I'm sure you've observed.'

He couldn't help but notice the way her hands shook as she beat her familiar rhythm on the tabletop.

He leant in, trying to relax his posture to make it clear he wasn't judging her in any way. 'It can't all be down to you. There'll be other factors too.'

He had no idea what they could be, but he needed to say something to take the look of abject misery off her face. He could imagine she'd be a challenging character to work for, but she wasn't cruel. At least not based on what he'd seen of her. Getting a team to work well together was a tough business, and it sounded as if she was having more than her fair share of trials at work. No wonder she was so exhausted. He shouldn't have made that crack about a nervous breakdown; it sounded as if he hadn't been far off hitting on the truth.

'I have a real talent for making people uncomfortable.'

She didn't seem to be able to make eye contact with him any more.

'I take out my temper on them. I should be nicer and more forgiving of mistakes, according to your sister. My PA usually takes the brunt of my anger.' She paused and spread her hands out on the table, staring down at her fingers before correcting herself. '*Took* the brunt.'

'And my sister asked you to take some time away?' He allowed himself to recognise a begrudging respect for Abi. Kudos to her for dealing with this problem head-on.

'Yeah, before I scare the rest of the team into quitting. I agreed to it because I needed to convince your sister I'm not losing my mind.'

'Are you?'

She huffed out a frustrated laugh. 'It feels like it some days. But work is all I have. It's important to me to be successful. I've worked so hard for it.' She gave a weak smile, but her lip wobbled and her eyes flicked down away from his gaze.

There was a tight feeling across his chest and he had to take a deep breath to release the tension. It was hard seeing her come undone, even though she clearly needed to say all this out loud, but he also felt a ridiculous surge of pleasure that he'd finally been able to get it out of her.

'So Abi's running the business by herself while you're here?'

'Yeah. Crazy woman. It's not like *she's* not stressed to her eyeballs too. She's the one who should be taking a holiday.' She closed her eyes and let out a low breath. 'I guess I just made things worse.'

A sudden sinking feeling in his gut at the thought of his sister dealing with the same anxiety distracted him. He needed to turn this conversation upside down before he got sucked into the melancholy that was nibbling at the edges of his consciousness. A game-changer was in order.

'Well, you know what's good for stress?'

'Enlighten me.'

'Orgasms.'

The word hung in the air between them, throbbing with potential life.

Her face was a picture. 'Did you just suggest that we…?' Josie waved a shaky finger between them both.

'That we waggle our fingers at each other?' he said, barely managing to keep the grin off his face at her stupefied reaction.

She tried to laugh but it came out as a cross between a hiccup and a snort. 'That you and I…?'

He leant in to her again, totally unable to control his urge to tease her. She was such an easy target, and the change in the atmosphere was a relief after the angst of their last conversation. 'You seem a little lost for words there, Josie. Are you asking me to have sex with you?'

She blushed fiercely and the sight of it made him smile. '*No!* I thought you were asking *me*.'

He paused, gathering his thoughts. What the hell was he doing? Whatever it was, he didn't feel like pulling back. 'What if I was?'

She shuffled in her chair. 'Well…that would be…a strange request.'

'Strange, unnatural? Or strange, I've-never-been-propositioned-so-directly-before?'

'The second one.'

He could imagine. She'd be an intimidating prospect. 'You haven't lived.'

'So you keep telling me.'

'I call it like I see it.'

'I've noticed.' She let out a loud sigh, as if she'd run out of steam, her shoulders slumping.

He frowned, feeling her change in mood. Her fire had gone out. 'You sure you're okay?'

She gave him a pained smile. 'I suspect I've not been entirely impressive since we met.'

'Oh, I don't know. Your tits are quite something.'

She crossed her arms and gave him a stern look. 'You know, you've only been able to get away with saying things like that because you're so big.'

He gave her a flattered smirk.

'I'm talking about your immense height and build, not...you know...' She nodded vaguely towards his crotch. The pink flush that appeared high on her cheeks made him grin.

"You know, for someone with such an extensive vocabulary you're woefully lacking in the dirty word department.'

She pulled her arms tighter across her body. 'I can swear with the best of them.'

'Sure you can.'

'Are you challenging me?' Tipping her chin up, she gave him that sexy rebellious stare that always made him hard.

Okay, that did it.

'Come with me,' he said, getting up and heading straight for the patio doors that led into the garden.

After a moment he heard the happy-making slap of her flip-flops on the path behind him as he strode past the terrace towards the bottom of the land.

CHAPTER FIVE

'WHERE ARE WE going?' Josie panted behind him as she tried to keep up.

'To the edge of nowhere.'

They reached the fence that bordered the farmhouse's land a minute later. The sun was setting in the distance, bathing the landscape in a soft crimson glow. The lavender fields glowed cerise in the dissolving light.

Stopping to lean on the fence, Connor gazed around him, luxuriating in the last flush of heat that rose from the land.

'What are we doing here?' Josie asked beside him, sounding a little nervous.

He turned to look her dead in the eyes. 'We're emoting. It's a trick I learned a while ago to help relieve stress.'

'Seriously?' She looked at him as if he was crazy.

'Come on, Josie, show me what you've got.'

She raised a sceptical eyebrow. 'We *are* still talking about the same challenge, right?'

He smiled. 'I want you to shout out as many swear words as you can think of. Loud as you like.' He wanted to see that fire back in her eyes and he knew that the only way to do that was to get her to let go of the anxiety she was lugging about with her.

She gave him a perplexed frown. 'Here?'

'Yup.'

She side-eyed him, folding her arms across her chest. 'I'd look like an idiot.'

'I won't point and laugh.'

'Are you sure? You haven't set up a camera out here, hoping to record my shame, have you?'

'Stop being so paranoid and get on with it.'

Her face was already pink with anticipated embarrassment, but there was a glimmer of life in her eyes again.

Was she going to do it? Or would she wimp out? He had no idea which way this would go.

He was about to find out.

Screwing her eyes up tightly, she took a deep breath, shoved back her shoulders and let rip, shouting a long and truly comprehensive list of dirty words into the ether.

Birds rose into the air in a distant field, startled by the noise.

She turned back to him and he gave her an awestruck nod. 'Impressive.'

Her face was bright red and her chest heaved as she gasped breath back into her body, but she beamed with pleasure, her eyes alive and clear, and at that moment he thought she looked like the most beautiful woman on earth. His heart hammered in his chest and his hands twitched at his sides. He wanted to pull her to him and kiss those soft-looking lips, draw out the remaining poison of her humiliation and set her conscience free.

Josie couldn't quite believe she'd just yelled a string of profanities into the tranquil stillness of the French landscape. What was happening to her? She appeared to be turning into a total nutjob, but she felt strangely light and floaty, as if she'd broken free of something. She felt good. Better than she had in a very long time.

'Pretty rushy, huh? That's the serotonin kicking in,' Connor said, his voice strangely rough and deep.

'Whatever it is, I want more,' she said, giving him a grin, no longer worried about embarrassing herself. She figured she'd stepped *waaay* over that line already.

'Me first, then you again,' he said, holding up a hand before tipping his head back to the sky and yelling his own wide-ranging string of racy expletives into the air, fists clenched at his sides.

He looked back at her, his eyes alive with laughter and something else she couldn't quite put her finger on.

'Your turn.'

'Okay.' She took a step back, taking a run-up. 'These are for you, Connor.' She took a deep breath, braced her hands against the fence, and belted out all the words she'd called him in her head since he'd gatecrashed her holiday.

When she finally looked back at him he was clearly trying not to laugh.

'Feel better?' he asked.

'Actually, I do.' She was shocked to find she was actually having fun.

'It's good to let go of that tension, right?'

'Yes, Dr Preston.'

He chuckled at that, then looked directly at her, the intensity in his bright blue eyes making her insides jump.

'Well, you need to get rid of that anger somehow. I'm guessing that's what gives you all that nervous energy.'

He took a step closer to her, triggering an immediate explosion of excitement deep inside her body. 'You need an outlet, but working hard obviously isn't doing it for you.'

She took a step away from him, uncomfortable with both her physical reaction and his sudden change of conversational direction. 'Go on, then, give me your conclusion, *Herr* Freud,' she said, bracing herself for some more home truths. He seemed to think he knew her better than she knew herself, but there was so much she hadn't told him. Maybe if everything were out in the open she'd be able to stop dodging his probing comments.

He dipped his head thoughtfully. 'What's it like, living under your sister's shadow?'

His question rattled her, but she knew there was no backing away from it. 'You think you've got me pegged, don't you?'

He ignored her.

'Tell me about it.'

It was easier to give in at this point. There was no way he was going to leave her alone until the whole sordid mess was out in the open.

Her legs shook with a mixture of nerves and lust, so she sat down to avoid collapsing in a puddle at his feet. Leaning her back against the fence, she waited for him to slide down next to her before she spoke.

'Okay, yes, you've got me. I'm the second favourite daughter in the family.' She glanced across at him but he was staring at his hands. 'I couldn't figure out what I was doing wrong when I was younger. I wanted my achievements noted, just like Maddie's were, but no matter what I did she outshone me. I was dim in comparison to her. I gave up trying to get any attention after a while and they sort of left me to it. I think they've all written me off as a failure.'

She tried to keep her voice light and breezy, but gave herself away at the end with a wobble on the last word.

Connor chose to ignore it, saving her from embarrassment. 'Even though you're running your own business?' he asked.

'They think I'm playing at it because it's taken a while

for us to get any traction in the marketplace. Abi and I spent a long time not taking a wage.'

'That's a tough thing to comprehend for anyone without a head—or the guts—for business.'

She pulled a long stem of grass out of the earth and ripped strands off it, keeping her fingers busy to stop herself digging her nails painfully into her palms. 'Every time I turn up at their house they ask the same polite questions about what's going on with the business and I have to give them the same answers and see the same look of boredom and disappointment on their faces. They want me to be so much more than I am.'

'Your sister's set an impossible standard.'

She let out a harsh shout of laughter and wagged a shaking finger at him. 'There is no such word as *impossible*, Connor. Not according to my father anyway.' She let out a long breath and tried to release the tension in her shoulders.

'What do they want you to be doing?'

'Something exciting and world-changing.'

'Why did you choose the business you did?'

'Because when I met Abi through a friend of a friend, and she talked to me about her ideas, I felt inspired for the first time in my life. And luckily she thought I'd make a good business partner. She's a great MD—all the staff love her. She has a way of motivating people and she's taken risks on giving people responsibilities that bring out the best them. That's something she and I disagreed on for a while, but it seems to have worked out pretty well so far. No one wants to disappoint her.'

'Least of all you?'

She smiled sadly. 'Too late for that.'

'I'm sure my sister knows how lucky she is to have

you working with her. It was a good move to surround herself with smart people.'

Josie snorted.

'What? You don't think you're smart?'

'I know I'm smart. Just not smart enough—or maybe not smart in the right way.'

'How do you quantify that? What does "smart enough" look like?'

'It looks solid, razor-sharp and Technicolor.' She relaxed her clenched hands to form a cage, as if she could somehow capture this elusive beast. 'Whole.'

Now she'd started talking she wanted to tell him everything—about all her fears and uncertainty and anger—but she knew she couldn't. He wouldn't want to hear it. Why should he? They weren't even friends. She bit her tongue.

He must have sensed her hesitation. 'Just say it, Josie. Say whatever it is you've been holding back. What's the worst that can happen?'

She took a deep breath. The words wanted to escape from her lips; she could feel them pushing to get out of her mouth.

Say it, Josie.

'I want to win. I want to bloody *win* for once, Connor. I'm so sick of second place.' She swiped at a speck of something in the air in frustration.

'Go on. Give it a shout-out.'

She let out a long, low sigh, pulling together the courage to do it.

'I want to *wiiiinnnn!*' Her fists were tight with tension and her body was rigid as she yelled it at the top of her lungs, eyes closed against the world.

There was a resounding silence as the echo of her

voice faded away into the dusk. Opening her eyes slowly, she saw Connor was looking at her intently.

'It's going to be fine, you know. You'll work it out,' he said.

The kindness of his tone almost broke her. Tears welled in her eyes and her throat felt so tight she thought she might choke.

He leant in and gently stroked the back of his hand over her cheek, as if brushing off a stray eyelash. The gesture was so intimate and unexpected she gasped. His eyes were dark as they stared into hers, filled with concern, and her insides twisted.

She caught the fresh, masculine scent of him, mingling with the nearby lavender on the breeze. He smelt wonderful—earthy and hot and spicy. She wanted to lick him he smelled so delicious.

The intensity of his expression was unnerving, but she had no idea what to do next. Her body burned with need. How could he possibly want her after all she'd just told him?

The dying rays of the sun deepened the planes of his face and she watched in fascination as his lips moved towards hers.

He was so close to her she could almost feel the touch of his mouth against hers. He'd tilted his head to angle it down towards her, so they were on a level, and his eyes looked clearly into hers. Their breath mingled as his hands drew her face closer to his, trapping her.

'What are you doing?' she whispered, forcing the words past her constricted throat.

He paused, his mouth only centimetres away from hers. 'I figure we're stuck here together, in the middle of nowhere for a week, without much to distract us,' he murmured. 'It seems like happenstance that we're both here right now, and I really, *really* want to kiss you.'

Her heart thumped against her chest. 'Happenstance?'

'Okay, sheer dumb luck.'

'I think your sister may have something to say about that.'

At the mention of his sister his shoulders slumped and he sighed, pressing his forehead against hers.

Way to break the mood, Josie.

God, what was she like? She knew she was a useless flirt. It had always felt counter-intuitive to flirt with men when she'd spent so many years battling with them to establish her position in the business world, but that was just an excuse.

She was afraid of what was happening here. This was Abigail's brother—a loner who didn't appear to care about anyone. The worst person in the world to be getting emotionally involved with.

She was terrified that once she gave in to these burgeoning feelings for him it would be a slippery slope down to disappointment. She really didn't need to add Connor to the long list of her mistakes. She needed to maintain her focus in order to get her life back on track. Connor was going to ruin that by kissing her. She was sure it wouldn't really mean anything to him. He just felt sorry for her. It would be a mercy kiss.

He moved his forehead away and for a second she thought he'd changed his mind—given her a reprieve—but he hadn't. He moved his mouth closer to hers again, until their lips were barely touching, sending tingling currents of pleasure across her skin.

'Wait,' she whispered against his mouth, closing her eyes so she didn't have to see the pity she felt sure must be there. But he didn't wait. He crushed his lips against hers, taking her breath away.

Her veins filled with fire as the kiss deepened, his lips insistent against hers. Strong fingers stroked along her arms and round to her back, drawing erotic circles against her skin. Waves of longing ripped through her and she instinctively opened her mouth against his, letting him in.

With a groan of pleasure Connor traced his tongue gently against hers, probing the soft depths of her mouth. His body was wrapped tight against hers, and his arms were pulling her into the dip of his body as he pushed her down to the ground. Taut muscles pressed against her belly and with a shock she became aware of his erection hard against her.

Frustration swamped her. She was being torn in two. Her body was telling her one thing and her mind another. She wanted him—there was no doubt about that—and yet it would be a disaster to go any further. She knew it. But couldn't she…for a short while…let herself have a bit of fun? That was all it would be. She couldn't see Connor wanting any more from her—not if he was as emotionally closed as he appeared. But— oh, God—she didn't want this to stop. His mouth was hot against hers, softer now she was yielding to him, but just as persistent.

Instinctively she moved her hands to scoop around his shoulders, feeling the tense muscles move beneath her touch. The strength of him frightened her.

The last remaining sane part of her brain gave her a kick. *No.* She had to stop this.

She put her hands against his chest and pushed. It was like trying to move a brick wall. His hands tightened around her for a second, then relaxed, setting her free.

Shuffling back out from under his body, she forced herself to look at him. He gazed at her, a deep frown marring his rugged face.

'What's wrong?' His breath came out in short gasps as he tried to regain his cool.

'We shouldn't be doing this. It's crazy. I can't afford distractions right now.'

Connor raised a questioning eyebrow. 'I think distraction is exactly what you need.' He leant in towards her again, bracing himself on both arms above her, and brushed his lips against her jaw.

Josie found she could barely speak. 'I don't have time for them,' she struggled out.

'It seems to me you have plenty of time.' His mouth moved down to caress the pulse point on her neck.

'No. I need to be thinking straight. I can't be side-tracked by a relationship.'

He drew back and looked at her, a frown creasing his brow. 'Wait a second. At what point did I ask you for a *relationship*?'

Josie blushed fiercely at her slip.

Rolling to the side, and anchoring himself on one forearm and one hip, he tucked a loose strand of hair behind her ear before running a finger gently along her jawline. This simple action sent shocks down her throat and deep into her highly sensitised body. She could barely concentrate on their conversation; he was upping the static in her already befuddled brain.

She pushed away from him again, giving herself the physical distance she needed to be able to think straight.

Her lips were still tingling from his punishing kiss and they gave a sudden throb, distracting her for a second. Bringing her hand up to her mouth, she could feel how swollen it was. She caught him watching her fingers as they brushed against her lips and his own parted as if in recognition.

Connor wanted to kiss her again, to hold her soft body against him, to break down those ironclad barriers.

He'd thought he could fight the urge to touch her, to kiss her, but he'd been wrong. When it came to Josie it seemed he had no willpower.

She'd seemed so lost, sitting there gazing up at him with her beautiful troubled eyes, and he'd found he couldn't bear it. Kissing her had seemed the only option.

She was one of those people who needed a push to cross her imaginary boundaries and he wanted to see that control break, for her to surprise herself with what she could do when she gave herself permission to ignore the rules she clung so tightly to.

He knew there was no future in this. She was too work-focused and he wasn't going to be around for much longer. But that hadn't stopped him kissing her. There wouldn't be enough time for an affair with her to become a problem, he assured himself. Anyway, perhaps he was doing some good here? The emoting had already yielded spectacular results.

'I'm sorry,' she said, her voice tight. Sitting up and pushing her shoulders back, she looked him directly in the eye, as if to challenge him to defy her.

'Why?'

Josie's discomfort was evident: her fingers drummed against the ground and she scuffed her toes through the grass. She clearly needed a little push in the right direction, but logical argument was his only option.

'You know why,' she said.

He sat back on his haunches and ran a hand through

his hair, gaining a moment to collect himself. 'Okay, Josie, listen. Let's cut the bull. We can dance around each other for the rest of the week, or we can be honest and stop wasting the little time we have together. I like you. You're a bit strange and uptight, and far too wrapped up in your career, but, hell, everyone's got their down sides.' He waited until she caught his eye, and then grinned.

Josie reluctantly smiled back. 'Thanks,' she said dryly.

'Seriously...' He took a breath. 'We're totally wrong for each other, but I reckon we both understand what's going on here. We don't have a future. We live in different worlds. But we do have a connection.'

He put his hand out to rub his thumb gently along her jawbone and felt her quiver beneath his touch.

Vindicated.

'The whole point of this holiday was for you to step away from reality, right?' he said, dropping his hand down to her waist and moving his thumb in gentle circles around her hip bone.

'I guess.' Her breath came out in irregular gasps. She didn't seem to be able to meet his eyes.

'So go with it.'

Josie couldn't look at him. She didn't want him to see how weak she was, how very near the edge. Instead she watched her own hand as she moved it to Connor's chest and felt his heart beating against her fingertips.

It picked up its pace, mirroring her own.

She knew this was a dangerous game she was playing, but something inside her had taken over. Her heart flipped. What was she getting herself into?

He moved forward, his eyes capturing hers, and raised his hand to tip her chin so her mouth was lined up with his own. She felt the vibration of his breath on her lips.

'I think you're cheating yourself, Josie. I think you want me as much as I want you.'

The truth was she was terrified she wouldn't be able to handle the heartache that was sure to come with any sort of emotional attachment to Connor. And she *would* get attached to him. So easily. If she let herself. He'd already made her feel things she hadn't experienced before, things she couldn't even begin to explain.

It was decision time.

Her body gave a throb of longing, as if trying to tell her which way to go. She thought about how long it had been since she'd been so attracted to someone and how few treats she'd allowed herself in the past few years. How hard she'd worked for very little return.

To hell with it. She'd let events take their course. She could handle a fling with him—she'd have to. The prospect of not having him now seemed so much worse than anything a short fling would do to her. At least she knew that was all it would be; she was going in with her eyes open. After all, she deserved some excitement in her life. She had nothing left to be afraid of. He already knew the worst of her and he was still here; that had to count for something.

'You want this too,' he said, his gaze raking her face. 'Don't you?'

'Yes.' She was shocked by how forcefully the word left her mouth.

'Good. Come with me.'

Standing up, he offered her his hand and she put hers inside it, gripping him tightly in her excitement. He pulled her to stand as if he was lifting a feather. Without another word he walked quickly back to the farmhouse, towing her with him, his long strides eating up the distance so she had to take two steps to his every one.

As soon as they made it inside he dragged her upstairs into the bedroom, slamming the door closed behind them.

Josie stood there, unsure what to do or say next, the blood pounding in her ears, her body humming with expectation. The air between them hung heavy with promise.

'So, Josie...'

His deep voice cut through the fuzziness in her head.

'You're sure you can handle a fling with me?'

Taking a ragged breath, Josie drew herself up to her full height. 'Of course I can.'

Before she registered what was happening Connor moved towards her, pushing her against the wall and trapping her within the cage of his body. He looked down at her, searching her face, his eyes alive with lust.

'You sure you've got time for me right now?' His voice was low and smooth and resonated through her bones.

Josie tipped her chin to look at him with as much poise as she could muster—which wasn't much. She was in over her head here. He was the quintessential man: powerful, self-contained and in control. And he knew it.

'I think I have a window.' Her words came out a little breathlessly, as if she'd just run a mile. His nearness was making her body react in strange ways. Her chest squeezed at her lungs, reducing their capacity and making her feel light-headed, and the space between her legs throbbed in anticipation of what was to come.

She gasped as his hand cupped her chin firmly, his thumb gently stroking against her mouth, causing it to open against the pressure of the movement.

'Let's see if we can't distract that big brain of yours for a while.'

Bringing his lips down hard onto hers, he forced her

mouth open, his tongue sliding firmly against hers. Stating his intent.

She let herself go and moved her mouth instinctively against his.

He was all around her, enveloping her senses. Every cell in her body wanted him closer, deeper, tighter. His hands grasped the back of her hair, holding her face to his. Escape would have been impossible. Not that she wanted that—now she'd finally surrendered to the inevitable she wanted it all.

Snaking her arms around his back, she ran her fingers up under his T-shirt to find the taut muscles and soft skin underneath. She heard him groan as her touch traced the bumps of his spine, then ran along the dips under his shoulder blades. Connor dragged his lips away from hers and yanked the T-shirt over his head in one swift movement, dropping it onto the floor next to him.

'Your turn,' he said, taking a step back to watch her.

She thought she'd feel self-conscious undressing in front of him, but his approving gaze made her bold. Slowly she slipped her T-shirt off, followed by her bra, until she stood there topless, mirroring him.

His gaze ran over her face, then down her neck to her breasts, where he lingered for a moment.

Josie's body pulsed with hunger for him.

Raising his hands to cup her breasts, he rubbed his thumbs gently over her nipples and she gasped as desire flooded her body, sending exquisite currents zinging to places she'd never realised could feel so turned on.

'You know, orgasms are good for headaches too. Something to do with endorphins,' he said, moving forward to kiss the sensitive spot behind her ear.

'You're offering to be my personal painkiller?' Her voice came out in a throaty gasp.

'It's a double win,' he murmured against her neck.

Moving his hands to grasp under her bottom, he lifted her off the floor and against him as if she weighed nothing.

Wrapping her legs around his waist, she pressed herself into his hard body, delighting in the feel of his erection against her stomach. She moved herself up and down against him, desperate to get closer, aching to feel him inside her.

Connor obviously wanted the same thing, because he spun around and carried her over to the bed, dropping her down onto soft pillows, his body pressing in on top of her. Their kissing was frantic now. It was such a release to be free of worry and to just let herself *feel*.

Connor shifted his position so he was kneeling above her. He broke the kiss and sat up, pulling her remaining clothes away in one swift movement, before tearing off his own and returning to kiss her.

'You're so beautiful,' he breathed against her mouth, dropping kisses along her cheek, onto her nose, across her forehead and closed eyes.

His tongue drew gentle circles against the outside of her ear, sending new tendrils of longing straight between her thighs. His fingers worked magic on her skin, teasing their way down her stomach to the top of her soft mound of hair. She arched towards him, desperate for his touch to move lower. It did, parting her folds to find the sensitive nub of her clit. With infinite care he swirled the pads of his fingertips against her, the rhythmical motion causing spasms of sweet, almost painfully intense sensation to rip through her. She moved against his touch, wanting more, wanting him deeper. Finally his fingers slid easily inside her, discovering how ready she was for him.

A groan erupted from her throat as he moved his fingers in and out, his thumb still circling the little bundle of nerves, the tips of his fingers massaging a sensitive spot of pleasure deep inside her.

She was vaguely aware of him moving down the bed, trailing hot kisses across the sensitised skin of her neck and breasts and grazing over the tingling peaks of her nipples, before moving lower to the dip of her belly button. His breath, hot against her already burning skin, sent shivers of pleasure to where his fingers worked, heightening the buzz he was already creating there. He moved his thumb from her throbbing clit and the heat of his mouth took over, sending an increasingly intense throb of sweet agony through her body.

His tongue flicked over and over the swollen nub while his fingers worked inside her, driving deeper and twisting inside to catch her sensitive G-spot on their way out.

Just when she thought she couldn't take any more he withdrew from her, bending away, leaving her startled and dismayed.

'What are you doing?' she nearly shouted.

He turned back with a devilish grin on his face. 'I'm getting protection,' he said, holding up his shorts, then extracting a condom from the wallet in his back pocket.

Josie exhaled hard in relief. For one awful moment she'd thought he was stopping, but Connor had no intention of doing such a thing. After rolling the condom on he was back with her, sliding between her legs, roughly pressing her thighs further apart. Their gazes locked, their faces only millimetres apart. The masculine smell of him invaded her senses, mingling with the sun-warmed scent of their skin.

'How much do you want me right now?' he teased.

She felt the tip of his erection pressing gently against

the slick opening to her. She wriggled, trying to push him inside.

He moved down, away from her. 'Answer the question, Josie.' His voice was ragged, as though he was struggling to keep it together, and the mere thought of seeing him lose his cool made her body throb with arousal.

'More than I've ever wanted anything.' She wasn't lying; she couldn't remember a time when she'd been so desperate to have something. She certainly hadn't ever wanted some*one* this much before.

'I want you to remember that feeling when you're back in your stuffy boardroom,' he whispered into her ear as he entered her, driving in hard and taking her breath away.

She had never fully connected with sex. She was too self-aware, too involved in her own head. Were the mechanics right? Was this the optimum position for a fast and satisfying orgasm? If she pressed this and tweaked that would it make her a better lover? The kaleidoscope of worries spinning through her head made her suddenly nervous. She *so* didn't want to get this wrong.

'Relax,' he murmured, obviously sensing her new tension.

Wiping her mind, she softened her muscles and let him take the lead, not allowing herself to think about how it was happening, only knowing that it was.

As Connor increased his pace they moved frantically together, each trying to draw out the ultimate amount of pleasure from the other, their bodies slippery in the heat.

Josie was lost in sensation like nothing she'd ever experienced before. The feel of his hard body pressed to her, trapped between her legs, was driving her wild. He smelt so good—so earthy and hot. His muscles moved under his soft skin, twisting and stretching beneath her fingertips, proving his strength to her over and over again.

Closing her eyes, she concentrated on the rasp of his stubble against her cheeks and the driving hardness inside her. His body was hitting sensitive spots over and over, until she couldn't have stopped moving against him if her life had depended on it.

Connor's increasingly powerful thrusts finally tipped her over the edge. Exquisite sensation spiralled out from within her, rushing through her body, sending a surge of blood through her ears and behind her eyes, turning her world black. She was only semi-aware of Connor reaching his own climax, before collapsing across her, holding her hard against him in a possessive embrace.

Connor lay with Josie beneath him, their limbs entwined, his body throbbing from the aftershock of his orgasm. It had been such an intense build-up with her that his body had thrown everything it had at satisfying his desperate need.

She wriggled beneath him and he levered himself up on his elbows to move his weight off her.

'Sorry, am I squashing you?'

She smiled up at him, a hazy look in her eyes. 'Squash away. I was quite enjoying being trapped here under you.'

He laughed, but pulled himself away from her into a sitting position, tugging off the condom. Josie reclined back against the pillows, her arms splayed above her head, her breasts rising gently in front of him. He wanted to kiss them, to take her rose-pink nipples in his mouth and gently bite them until she moaned.

So that was what he did, straddling her body and sliding a hand down to tease the soft skin of her thighs.

His body was ready for her again in an instant.

Somehow he'd known they'd end up like this. What he couldn't have guessed was how incredible it was going to be. Just how much he'd want her even now.

A vague discomfort pushed at the edge of his consciousness, but he ignored it in order to concentrate fully on Josie and her magnificent body.

She writhed beneath him, her pelvis tipped up, arching her back to try and make contact with him again.

He raised his head to look at her. 'So, was it worth it?'

'What?' Her voice sounded guttural after their exertions.

'Giving in to your instincts for a change?'

'*So* worth it.' She smiled and pulled his face towards hers, kissing him hard on the mouth.

She tasted so sweet. He could happily lose himself in the taste of her, the smell of her skin, the softness of her touch.

'I'm so glad I let you stay,' he said, stifling her laugh of protest with a kiss. Pulling away, he looked her in the eye. 'How's your head now?'

She gave him a quizzical frown. 'Are we talking about my pain level or my sanity?'

He laughed. 'Your headache.'

'Gone, thanks to your miracle cure.'

She snaked her arms around him, running her fingertips over his back, making the skin tingle where she touched him.

'Glad to hear it.'

She closed her eyes and exhaled sharply through her nose. 'This is *not* at all what I expected from my holiday when I arrived here.'

'It's turning out to be a pretty good break after all, huh?' He pushed a stray lock of hair off her forehead.

She opened her eyes and looked at him. 'I can't complain,' she said, her smile more relaxed than he'd ever seen it. Wriggling up the bed, she extricated herself from the cage of his body and moved to sit up.

'I don't know if my legs are going to hold me.' She grinned sheepishly at him.

'Where are you going?'

That couldn't be it, surely? The thought of being packed off downstairs to sleep made his stomach sink. He'd hoped this had only been the prelude to a long night of exploring Josie's remarkably responsive body.

'Bathroom.'

'Well, hurry back,' he said, flipping onto his back. He smiled as her gaze slid down his torso and she raised an amused eyebrow.

'As you can see, I'm not finished with you yet,' he said. 'Not even close.'

CHAPTER SIX

WHEN JOSIE WOKE the next morning it took a few seconds for the events of the previous day to rush back. Heat swept through her, bringing with it a crushing mixture of embarrassment and lust.

Had she really yelled expletives across the calm French landscape and then shagged her business partner's estranged brother? She wouldn't be surprised to find she'd dreamed it. It was all so surreal.

Sitting up, she took a slow breath before turning to look at Connor, sleeping soundly next to her. He was lying on his side, facing her, his top arm slung forward across his bare chest. In the semi-darkness she could only just make out the contours of his face, his strong jaw and high cheekbones, the slash of his eyebrow.

He was quite something to look at.

She allowed herself to imagine for a second what it would be like to wake up next to him every day. The thought made her tremble. He unnerved her. He definitely wasn't the type of guy she usually went for. He was too unpredictable, too unstable. She liked men she could feel secure around. Men she could control. And that wasn't Connor by any stretch of the imagination.

It had been an oddly cathartic experience, talking to him about what had happened at work, and he'd been really sweet about it, but she was furious with herself for letting her guard down like that. What must he think of her? And the sex. Oh, God, the hot, desperate, messy sex. She'd been totally out of her mind last night.

Shuffling to the edge of the bed and swinging her legs out slowly, she found she was twitchy and on edge. How was one supposed to act after a night of hot sex with a virtual stranger? She had absolutely no idea.

Grabbing some clean underwear, a pair of shorts and a vest top, she quietly left the room so as not to wake him. She needed a strong cup of coffee and some time to compose herself before she faced him again.

After taking a speedy shower in the bathroom she swiped mascara onto her lashes and took stock of herself in the mirror. The sun had turned her usually creamy skin a subtle honey colour and she was pleased to see it rather suited her. She could almost pass for healthy-looking.

Down in the kitchen, she was watching the last bit of coffee drip into the jug when she heard a noise behind her and turned to find Connor leaning against the doorjamb. He'd put on a pair of shorts, but he was still bare-chested.

Her heart nearly leaped out of her body at the sight of him.

When she was finally able to drag her gaze up from where the perfectly contoured triangle of his hips disappeared into the top of his shorts she attempted to focus on his face. Had she really kissed him all over last night, running her tongue along the lines that delineated his muscles and ending up somewhere very delicious indeed? It was almost impossible to look him in the eye with those memories flashing through her mind.

'Morning,' she said. Playing it cool was the only way to deal with this. She hoped.

He smiled in an I-know-just-what's-going-through-that-dirty-mind-of-yours way and ran a hand through his bedhead hair.

Her mind flicked to the image of him asleep. The look of peace on his strong face had made him seem more vulnerable somehow, but there was no trace of that left now. He was back to being the bear of a man she was used to.

'Morning, Josie. How's your head today?' he said.

Clearly he was having no problem whatsoever with the fact that they'd screwed each other silly last night. She envied him his total imperturbability.

'Fine. Good. It's not…er…it's fine. Thanks.'

Where had her power of speech scurried off to?

Connor grinned and sauntered over to where she was hovering by the coffee maker. Leaning across, he grabbed the jug and poured them both a mugful before handing one to her without a word.

She leant back against the worktop, grateful for its sturdiness in the face of her sudden inability to support her own body weight. She focused on him slotting bread into the toaster to calm herself. God, she loved how he moved.

How was she ever going to function normally in his presence again? She really needed to get things straight here before she lost her mind.

'So, what happens now?' she asked, casually flicking her hair over her shoulder and simultaneously sloshing coffee onto the floor by her feet.

'We drink coffee.' He glanced down at the floor in amusement. 'Preferably out of our mugs.'

'No, I mean how is this going to work? You and I?' she asked, ignoring a hot flush of embarrassment.

He turned to look at her and smiled. 'Do you want me to write you a schedule of events?'

Despite her awkwardness, Josie couldn't help laughing. 'That won't be necessary, thanks. I meant… Oh, I don't know what I meant. I have no clue what to think about all this.'

He moved to where she stood against the worktop and put one hand on either side of her body, trapping her. The heat of his presence warmed her clammy skin.

'Josie, relax. Stop trying to plan everything and just go with it.'

Leaning in, he kissed her nose. He smelt of sleep with an undertone of his own peppery scent.

Josie closed her eyes, allowing herself to enjoy the closeness of his body for a moment. She was uncomfortably aware that she needed to keep some part of herself aloof from him. He would be leaving soon and she needed to make it as easy on herself as possible.

'Okay, well, I'm going to go and make some more notes on that tender I was writing before I completely forget it,' she said on reflex, forgetting her decision to step away from work. It was a natural defence mechanism— a habit she'd developed when she needed to avoid the real world.

His body stiffened and he pushed himself away to arm's length. 'Josie…' There was a warning tone in his voice. 'If you want this holiday to do you some good you're going to have to keep your head out of work.'

'I—' she began.

'No work. No writing documents.'

There was a heavy silence while she considered the wisdom of his words. She really had no leg to stand on after what she'd told him last night.

'Yeah. Okay.'

He nodded and moved away as his toast popped up. She watched him spread it with butter and honey and wolf it down while she sipped her coffee. He even managed to make eating breakfast look sexy.

'So, what are your plans for the day? No more treks in the midday heat, I hope,' he said, breaking into her thoughts about what she'd love to do with the rest of that honey.

She cleared her throat before trusting herself to speak. 'I'm going to stay here today. I might even try some cooking. I hear it's relaxing.'

Connor nodded, raising a questioning eyebrow. He looked as if he was going to say something, then shrugged.

'Good luck with that,' he said at last. 'I'm going out.'

The disappointment nearly floored her.

'Oh. Okay.' She struggled to keep her voice level, not wanting him to see how much this affected her. Not even sure why it did. Just because they'd had sex, it didn't mean he was under any obligation to spend all his time with her. 'Have a good time,' she said lamely.

He ran a hand through his tousled hair. Turned as if to go. Turned back. 'You should come with me.'

Her head shot up. 'What?'

'Come to the beach with me. It might keep you out of trouble for a while.'

Excitement flooded through her, followed closely by unease. Perhaps she was pushing her luck here. He didn't really want her tagging along but obviously felt sorry for her.

'Maybe I should rest up here today?' she hedged.

'Be ready to go in half an hour.'

She glimpsed a hint of a smile in his eyes.

Before she had time to utter another word he turned and walked away, and she heard him mount the stairs, apparently taking them two at a time.

* * *

What had made him do that? Connor wondered as he showered. He'd been all set to get away from the house and clear his head when he'd done a complete U-turn.

What had happened with Josie last night had him spun. He'd felt an almost animalistic urge to protect her and the ferocity of the feeling had shocked him. She was obviously embarrassed today about what they'd done so he'd thought the kindest thing to do would be to give her some space.

It had been the look on her face, he decided, when he'd said he was leaving her alone, that had changed his mind. She'd looked so forlorn he hadn't been able to bring himself to do it.

She was obviously trying to hide the fact she wanted to go out to save face, but he could sense her desperation to leave the farmhouse. She was going to go stir-crazy on her own. Cold turkey was insanely difficult to handle when you didn't have company.

Besides, it would be more fun to go to the beach with someone else. It didn't have to mean anything. They were two people who just happened to have had sex, going to the beach for a change of scene. As he'd pointed out last night, it wasn't as if there was any future in this thing between them. It was a holiday fling—nothing more.

He dressed in khaki shorts and a light cotton T-shirt, grabbed his sunglasses and went to find Josie.

She was waiting for him in the kitchen, a bag at her feet, drumming her fingers against the tabletop. Was she playing a tune in her head? he wondered. The movement of her fingers reminded him of a pianist's.

'Do you play?'

She spun around, looking flustered. 'I'm sorry?'

'The piano? Do you play? You always seem to be tapping out a rhythm. I wondered if you were playing to yourself.'

She smiled. 'Nothing gets past you, does it?'

'Nope.'

'Actually, I do play, but I haven't for a while. I miss my piano.'

'Well, maybe we can do something about that.' He bent down and picked up her bag. 'Let's go.'

He clocked her confused expression and smiled to himself. Today could be fun.

His car was a cherry-red soft-top Triumph Stag. He loved it. He'd missed it whilst he was away and couldn't wait to take it out for a spin. Pulling back the dust sheet, he uncovered the gleaming bodywork and soft leather interior. It was a piece of art: characterful and stylish, unlike some of the garish sports cars that dominated the roads these days. This car was a gentleman amongst peasants.

He ran a loving hand over it before unlocking the doors and holding Josie's open for her. She'd noticed the caress and was smiling at him, an eyebrow raised.

'Nice car.'

'Thank you.'

She slid into the passenger seat and Connor caught a flash of her bare legs as she swung them in. He swore under his breath. What was he doing? He probably should have taken her straight back to bed instead of going along with this sham friendly trip to the seaside. Just a flash of her shapely calves had sent his responses into overload, and now he had to endure over an hour in close proximity with her without being able to take advantage of the fact.

Too late now.

He took his time clipping down the soft top of the roof

to give his body a chance to settle down, before striding round to the driver's seat and sliding in next to her.

'You'd better cover your hair for the journey,' he said, leaning across her to open the glove compartment. He kept his hand as far away from her legs as he could, acutely aware that temptation was a mere five centimetres away.

He pulled a scarf roughly out of the glove compartment and tossed it to her.

'Nice.' She looked at the scarf, then at him, a mirthful eyebrow raised. 'Hermes. Not the sort of item I'd expect to find in your possession. Is there something you want to tell me?'

Her eyes were full of laughter. It was lovely to see her lightening up a bit.

'Very funny.' He smiled back. 'It belonged to an old girlfriend. I forgot to throw it away.'

'Really? Throw it away? Not give it back? Sounds like it ended messily.'

He bridled, uncomfortable with the turn in conversation. 'Yeah,' he said gruffly, 'it did.'

They both shifted in their seats.

'Have you been split up for long?'

'About a year.' He stared at the steering wheel, unwilling to allow this conversation to develop.

'Katherine, right?'

He could sense her looking at him intently.

'You thought I was her in your bed the other night, didn't you?'

He *so* didn't want to be talking about Katherine right now. He nodded curtly, hoping she'd drop the subject.

'Why did you split up?'

He sighed, giving her a reproachful look, trying to

scare her off the subject. 'She wanted to get married, I didn't.' Hopefully that was the end of the inquisition.

'Why not?'

Apparently it wasn't. 'We were a bad fit.'

'Because she was looking for some stability?'

He gripped the steering wheel, the tendons in his hands tensing against the pressure.

'I didn't want it enough.'

'You love your freedom more?'

'Can we drop the subject?' he snapped, making her jump. He hated having to explain to new partners why his previous relationships had failed. Not that Josie *was* a partner. She wasn't anything to him. Nothing at all.

'Okay, I'm sorry.' Josie held her hands up as a peace offering. 'I was being nosy. It's none of my business.'

Firing up the engine, he backed out of the garage, killing the conversation. Mercifully, the roar of the engine and the crunch of the wheels on the road made it difficult to talk again.

It took them an hour and a half to reach Cannes. They headed straight for the centre and parked up.

'Okay. Let's rock this place,' Connor quipped, unfolding his large frame from the car and running a hand through his windswept hair.

The streets were crowded with summer visitors out enjoying the sunshine. They wove through them to get to the tree-lined Croisette, which was bordered on one side by the calm, sparkling Mediterranean Sea and on the other by some of the most exclusive hotels in the South of France.

'Wow, this is amazing,' Josie said, looking around in awe.

Connor glanced over at her. 'You like?'

'Sure do. Where are we going first?' She couldn't keep the excitement out of her voice. This place was something else—vibrant with life and humming with possibility.

'The Carlton Hotel. I need a drink.'

Josie would have preferred to head straight to the beach, but she didn't want to get separated from him and find herself stranded. She'd decided in the car to go with whatever flow Connor chose today. That strategy seemed to have worked out pretty well so far.

Connor strode through the crowds, which parted to make way for him. He had such a dominating presence Josie wasn't surprised people didn't want to get in his path. There was a defiance about him that seemed to act like a force field, and apparently she wasn't the only one to feel it. It felt good to walk beside him, as if he was her own private bodyguard.

They passed rows of designer shops, their windows all dressed with cutting-edge couture. Josie slowed down to gape at some of the crazy fashion on show.

'Want to go shopping?' Connor asked, a look of patent dread on his face.

She shook her head. 'No, thanks. I suspect I'd regret paying five hundred euros for a T-shirt that'll be out of fashion in a month.'

He swiped an exaggerated hand over his brow, the relief evident on his face.

They approached the magnificent frontage of the Carlton Hotel and he led her in through the terrace, where groups of fashionistas were soaking up the rays whilst sipping elegant-looking cocktails. Josie squeezed past the crowded tables, feeling the eyes of the patrons on her. Her earlier euphoria at being here evaporated. Dressed as she was, in shorts and a vest, she felt totally out of place. It had been so long since she'd gone to a bar like this one she'd forgotten how self-conscious they made her feel.

She was surprised Connor had chosen this place. Based on what she knew of him so far, she would have thought he'd be more at home in a dark, anonymous pub. But then she suspected she didn't *really* know him. He hadn't shown her his real self. It was all front and no substance. There was a private self in there somewhere that he wasn't allowing out.

Josie followed Connor into the grand lounge, stopping at the entrance to take in the magnificent sight that met her while Connor went to the bar.

The high ceilings and large windows allowed the summer sun to flood into the room, striking the large pillars that ran through the middle of the space and reflecting light back from the subtle creams and yellows of the decor. Large chandeliers hung majestically above art-deco-inspired seating arrangements that were sparsely populated due to the lure of the sunlit terrace outside. The clientele obviously came to the Carlton to be seen rather than to appreciate the beautiful architecture of the building. A large black-lacquered grand piano in the middle of the room caught Josie's eye and she became aware of her fingers as they twitched at her sides.

Connor approached carrying two drinks and handed one to her.

'Champagne cocktail.'

The way he said it was halfway between an order and a dare. There was no way he was letting her get away with not drinking the proffered drink.

'Are you trying to get me drunk?'

Connor smiled. 'On one glass of champagne? Surely it takes more than that to get the better of you?'

He kept a straight face but the innuendo hung between

them. Josie's stomach did a double backflip as images from the night before ran through her mind. It had taken precious little persuasion to get the better of her *then*.

'It takes a *lot* more than that,' she bluffed, taking the drink from him with a slow smile. It was such fun flirting with him. 'Thanks.'

He watched as she took a tentative sip and a shot of pure pleasure fizzed through her veins.

She didn't normally drink much, having always been too busy to allow her control to slip and deal with the consequences. She didn't have time for partying and hangovers, but all those curtailed birthday parties and missed nights out had left her with a dwindling base of friends whom she barely spoke to any more. She felt a twinge of shame at the thought. That definitely wasn't something she was admitting to Connor.

'Okay,' he said, once she'd taken another sip, 'go and play.'

'What?' Was he crazy?

'The piano. Go and play. I know you're desperate to. I saw that look of longing when you first came in.'

'I can't just sit down in a hotel lounge and start playing their piano.' Her heart pounded at the thought of it. She never played for other people; it was something very private to her.

'Of course you can.'

He took the drink from her quivering hand and gently pushed her towards the piano, his palm in the small of her back. Her skin burned under his touch.

'No. Connor. Seriously, I can't. I don't play in public. I'm not that good.' Her voice wobbled with nerves.

'Who's going to care?' He gestured towards the one remaining couple in the lounge. They were deep in conversation at the other side of the room.

'I know the bar staff here. They said it's fine. Go ahead.'

Josie weighed up her options. There weren't any. If she flat-out refused to play she'd ruin the companionable atmosphere they'd tentatively started to build between them. And if she was really honest with herself she did want to play; her fingers ached to touch the beautiful ivory keys, to caress their polished surface and make them sing. If only Connor wasn't there watching her she'd be able to step out of herself and get lost in the music for a while.

She glanced up at him and he gave her a reassuring smile.

To hell with it. It didn't matter what he thought. After last night there wasn't much of herself left to expose to shame anyway.

'Okay.' She sat down on the stool and made herself comfortable.

He simply nodded and took a seat at a nearby table, twisting his glass between his fingers as he waited for her to start playing.

She felt his gaze on her as she collected her thoughts and tried to blank his presence out of her consciousness.

Not an easy task, given that her skin seemed to prickle with energy whenever he was nearby. He was not a man you could easily ignore.

The keys were cool and smooth under her fingers and she revelled in the sensation of them against her skin for a moment. She smiled to herself before moving her hands across the ivories.

Connor sat back in bemusement as the theme tune to *The Simpsons* flowed from beneath Josie's fingers. That was the very last thing he'd expected her to play. He'd antici-pated a well-executed piece of classical music to fit with the sombre atmosphere of the bar, but she'd gone for a comic, upbeat tune instead, almost in defiance of her surroundings. She was clearly teasing him.

Once again she'd proved herself to have hidden depths. He was beginning to doubt his judgement. Reading people was usually one of his strengths, but he was having real trouble with Josie. She surprised him at every turn.

She'd tied her hair back from her face today, and he watched her slim neck and shoulders glide from side to side as her fingers danced over the keys. The anxiousness in her body was gone, leaving only grace and elegance. It was a beautiful thing to watch.

Glancing back, she gave him a cheeky smile before seguing into a composition by Philip Glass— *Metamorphosis One*, a fitting choice. It was a haunting melody, heavy with longing. Mesmerised, he stared at her as she moved with the music, seemingly oblivious to anyone or anything else. He envied her that total absorption.

As he listened the music affected him in strange ways. Memories of them together in the farmhouse ran through his head: her delight at beating him at chess; the way she'd looked in just her underwear after he'd brought her in from the heat; how she'd felt in his arms when she'd finally started to trust him. His body stiffened at the memory and his throat grew tight.

Out of the corner of his eye he noticed a small crowd of people begin to drift in from the terrace outside to listen to her play.

Jealousy hit him like a punch to the gut.

He didn't want anyone else to be here. It was as if they were invading something private that was taking place between him and Josie. This performance should be just for him.

Unnerved again by the strange possessiveness he felt

about her, Connor mentally shook himself and took another swig of his drink. What the hell was happening to him?

His pulse raced in his veins and his body temperature had risen to the point where he was drenched with perspiration. A heavy dread pulled at his head, like a lead weight dragging him down to the ground. Was this a panic attack? He hadn't had one for years but he recognised the symptoms. His heart beat wildly in his chest and his breath caught painfully in his throat. He needed to get out of there—get some air and put some distance between them before she noticed what was happening to him.

Josie only became aware of her audience as she neared the end of the piece. She blushed fiercely at the attention, but managed to keep her concentration. Now was not the time to get the notes wrong. Searching around surreptitiously, she noticed Connor sneaking off towards the terrace, with a hard, uncomfortable look on his face.

Mortification hit her stomach with a thump. He obviously wasn't impressed with her amateur attempt at a difficult piece of modern classical music. She'd pushed things too far, tried to be too clever, and she'd embarrassed herself—and him too, by the looks of it.

Even so, it was pretty rude to walk out before the end.

She clenched her arms hard to her sides, fighting an urge to slam the piano lid shut in her anger. It shouldn't matter if he didn't rate her playing, she reminded herself, but she realised with a slow, sinking sensation that she did care. She cared very much.

CHAPTER SEVEN

'OKAY, LET'S GO.'

Connor watched in surprise as Josie swept past him on the terrace, throwing the comment behind her without even a backward glance. Confusion and light-headedness from the attack made his reactions slow and it was a full five seconds before he realised she wasn't waiting for him.

She was striding towards the Palace de Festival, her body tense and upright and her head held high.

Pulling himself together, he jogged after her, catching her up at one of the entrances to the beach.

'Hey! Hey! Slow down. Where the hell are you going?' He had to walk fast to keep up with her.

Josie didn't even turn to look at him. 'For a walk.' She powered on, trying to outrun him, her neck and shoulders once again rigid and her face set in an angry frown.

'Josie, for God's sake, stop!' He managed to get ahead of her and block her path, forcing her to slow down.

She glared at him. 'Why did you make me do that?'

'What? Play?'

'Yes.'

'It was good. It was…very accomplished.'

'Sure—that's why you left before the end of the piece.'

'What? No... It wasn't because... Ah, hell.' He rubbed a hand over his eyes in frustration.

He'd just made everything so much worse. Now he owed her an explanation about why he'd walked out. How was he going to explain when he didn't even know why he'd reacted like that himself?

'Never mind. It doesn't matter.'

She held up her hand as if to bat away any excuse he gave her, smiling calmly now, her cool disdain making him feel even worse.

'I know I'm not that good. It must have been excruciating for you.'

Connor sighed and hooked his thumbs into the pockets of his shorts, his fingers curled hard into fists. 'Look. I'm sorry I left. I needed some air and I didn't think you'd mind. You seemed so engrossed.'

'I don't mind.'

She shrugged nonchalantly, but he detected a quiver in her voice.

Guilt slammed into him, bringing anger with it. His pulse beat a dangerously fast throb through his veins and his skin pricked with heat. There was nothing he hated more than feeling guilty.

Josie watched in dismay as Connor's eyes flared with irritation.

'What do you want from me? Want me to tell you again how amazingly talented you are?'

'No...no, of course not. I...' She was shaken by his coldness. 'I don't want anything from you.'

She did, though. She wanted him to be impressed; to tell her she was talented, attractive, smart. It mattered to her what he thought.

A hot flush made its way up her neck. She'd been so

overtaken with the joy of playing and losing herself in the music that she'd let her heart rule her head there for a while. She'd imagined that she and Connor were beginning to understand each other, but she'd been wrong. The disappointment weighed heavy.

They were both breathing rapidly from the fast pace she'd set and the side effects of their anger. Josie watched Connor's chest rise and fall, unable to look him in the face. She felt like an idiot. Again. Before meeting Connor she'd been the Queen of Cool around men, totally in control of her emotions and on top of every situation, and she'd stupidly thought she could handle him. But she was well out of her depth.

'Hey.' He moved in towards her, putting a hand lightly on her arm.

She looked up to see that the anger had drained from his face. A pulse beat in her throat as his gaze locked onto hers.

Josie took a deep breath. 'I want to go for a walk on the beach.'

She had to get away from his hypnotising gaze. If she didn't she'd probably end up making an even bigger fool of herself. She could still feel where his touch had brushed her arm. She ached for him to hold her again; she wanted that connection they'd had last night but had no idea how to get it back.

Connor nodded. 'Look, I'm sorry. I guess I'm on edge.' He rubbed a hand over his jaw. 'I'll come with you. A bit of fresh air would be good for us both right now.'

His mouth smiled, though his eyes didn't. Was he already regretting this fling? Her stomach writhed in discomfort, a mass of snakes slithering in her belly.

They took the next opening in the wall down onto the sand and strolled in silence for a while, listening to the rush of the waves against the beach. It was busy on the dry sand with sunbathing holidaymakers, so they walked next to the sea, where the ground was damp. Josie slipped off her shoes, finding relief in the coolness against the hot soles of her feet.

'How long have you been playing?' Connor asked, breaking the tense silence that had fallen between them.

'A few years.'

'Right.' He nodded. 'It had real warmth. It took me by surprise,' he said, not meeting her gaze but instead looking off out to sea. 'Your playing doesn't fit with the rest of you. It's like you let go of what keeps you so on edge.'

Josie stopped and looked at him, an eyebrow raised. 'That sounded suspiciously like a compliment. Except for the on edge bit.'

The corner of his mouth turned up and he huffed out a laugh. 'Look, I'm sorry, Josie. I've got a lot of stuff on my mind. I wasn't expecting all this.' He waved his hands around in the air.

'All what? This trip? Or the whole finding me naked in your bed thing?'

'The naked thing.' Throwing her a tight grin, he gestured to a free area of dry sand behind them. 'Want to sit for a minute?'

This all felt suspiciously as if it was leading up to a brush-off conversation and her skin prickled with nerves. Perhaps she should try nipping this whole thing in the bud first, to save them the awkward conversation he seemed to be building up to. She had to be in control of this thing or it had the potential to get messy very quickly.

She dropped onto the sand and grabbed a handful, concentrating all her attention on it as it flowed out through her fingers.

Be cool, Josie. Be cool.

'You know, it's fine if you don't want to take things any further. I understand. You're heading off soon and you're a busy man. Let's just call last night a glitch.'

He frowned. 'A glitch?'

'Yes.'

He was silent for a while.

'Abi's been such a good friend to me. I can't believe I shagged you when you won't even speak to her,' she said to cover the awkwardness, aiming for conviviality but failing miserably.

Connor's voice was hard. 'Who you shag has nothing to do with her.'

'But it seems so...disrespectful.'

He grinned at her and her stomach dropped to the ground.

'You're so prim. Don't get me wrong. I find it a huge turn-on.'

He really needed to stop flirting with her if he wasn't up for more shenanigans. Perhaps a question more close to the bone would remind him of that.

'Are you ever going to tell me *why* you won't see you own sister?'

He turned to study her for a second. 'You're not going to drop this, are you?'

'No.'

He continued to look at her, his eyes searching for something in hers—a trap, perhaps? She'd never met anyone so guarded.

'What the hell?' He shrugged. 'Makes no difference to me anyway.' He ran his fingers through his hair. 'You know about my parents?'

'Sure—they used to own the Magnetica Corporation.'

'Right. It used to be a thriving company. They made

cassette tapes, then video tapes, right up until the early nineties when they were all the rage.'

'Yeah, I remember seeing their adverts on TV at Christmas.'

Connor let out a low, hard laugh and dug his feet into the soft sand. 'Yeah, well... One of the reasons they were so successful was because both of my parents worked there all the time. And I mean *all* the time.'

He paused, but Josie didn't want to butt in. She let the silence hang, sliding her fingers through the sand for something to do.

'So Abigail and I spent most of our time with an ever-changing succession of nannies and au pairs. We were purely fashion accessories to our parents. We barely saw them, or each other. They sent us to separate schools. The only person who had any time for us was our grandmother. We spent our holidays with her. She left us the farmhouse in her will when she died. I was eighteen and Abigail was sixteen when we lost her. She didn't agree with the way our parents had brought us up—she believed children needed their mother and father. It caused a huge rift between them. They were practically estranged by the time she died.'

Josie nodded, eager for him to continue. This went part way to explaining why he was such an independent character and why he'd been so hard on her when they'd first talked about her career.

'Magnetica had started to lose money a little while before our grandmother died. The digital revolution was beginning and the stuff my parents manufactured was becoming obsolete. They'd planned poorly for the future and found themselves in money trouble. We, apparently, were their way out of debt. My grandmother was a rich woman—she just didn't flaunt it like my parents did.

She left most of her money to me and the remainder to Abigail, but left our parents nothing. I think they were banking on the inheritance to get their business out of trouble. So they put pressure on us to invest in their company. Nobody else would touch them with a bargepole. They wanted control of the money. We were in the way.'

'But you didn't agree to it?'

'I refused to help. My grandma had made Abigail and me promise not to give them a penny. It was really important to her they didn't get their hands on it. I already had plans for the money. I wanted to do some good with it. There were people starving in the world—dying from drinking filthy water, for God's sake. Personal entertainment didn't rank highly on my list of priorities.'

'So what happened?'

He dug his feet deeper into the sand. 'Abigail buckled under the pressure and agreed to use her share to help my parents out. She backed them up when they put pressure on me to do the same. Basically, it was made clear that if I didn't help them out financially I wouldn't be welcome in the family any more.'

Josie stared at him, aghast. 'That doesn't sound like the Abigail I know.'

Connor looked at her steadily. 'You think I'm lying?'

The tone of his voice was so scornful she felt a flash of alarm.

'Of course not,' she said hurriedly. 'I just can't reconcile it with the woman I know, that's all.'

He leant back on his elbows and looked out to sea. 'She had some crazy idea that my parents would suddenly realise what a crappy job they'd done raising us and it would all be rainbows and fairy dust if we handed over our inheritance. When I wouldn't, she stood back and watched them cut me out of the family.'

'I don't understand why Abi would do that to you.'

He shrugged. 'She wanted an easy life. And I guess she was jealous I'd got more of the inheritance than she had. Perhaps she was trying to level things out. I don't know.'

Josie stared at him. His face was expressionless, as if he'd locked his feelings about the whole mess down tight—as if this was just some ordinary story he was re-counting. His coldness disturbed her. If he could be this way about his family—the people he was supposed to love unconditionally—how would he deal with the ups and downs of a relationship with a lover? Another strike against him.

'And you've never spoken to any of them again?'

He shrugged. 'Abigail's tried to contact me over the years, but I'm not interested. She burnt that bridge long ago by siding with them.' His expression hardened, his brow furrowing and his lips thinning. 'My parents are dead now—but you knew that, right?'

Sitting up, he picked up a small stone and threw it hard into the sea, where it disappeared with a *plop.*

She nodded, remembering Abi having time off a year ago when her mother had passed away after losing her battle with cancer. 'Well, I imagine Abi regrets what happened now.'

'I should think so. The business went bankrupt so she'll have lost the lot.'

There wasn't a flicker of concern in his tone.

Josie knocked the sand off her hands and rubbed her fingers across her forehead to relieve the sudden pressure there, sadness surging through her for them both. How awful to be made to pick sides like that. No wonder he was so emotionally detached.

'Will you ever give Abi a chance to explain?'

'Why would I? I have no interest in seeing her again.'

She could see why Abi was resigned to him never letting her back into his life; he was so single-minded about it. This inflexibility unnerved her; it double-proved him to be a dangerous person to get involved with, but she still ached to be able to help both him and his sister in some way.

Her self-preservation mode kicked in before she had time to analyse her feelings fully.

'You really are one stubborn son of a bitch, you know,' she blurted, immediately regretting the bite of anger in her voice.

He just looked at her for a beat, then shrugged, his face blank of emotion. His ability to lock down so tight was chilling.

'Do you think we should end this thing between us?' she asked, bracing herself for the affirmative.

'Do you?'

She paused. On one hand she didn't think she could stand being around him, allowed only to look and not touch—not when she knew how great it could be with him. It would be torture. On the other it would be the shrewdest thing to do. She was already having trouble dealing with the crazy mess of emotion he was stirring in her and this was *not* what she'd signed up for.

Take control, Josie.

'Perhaps it would be for the best.'

He grunted and shook his head, then shrugged again. 'Fine.' Standing up, he offered her his hand and pulled her to stand. 'Let's go home,' he said wearily.

They were both quiet for the journey home. Connor had put the roof up on the car, enclosing them in their own uncomfortably intimate world. Without anything else to do, Josie ran over and over their earlier conversation in her head until she thought she'd go crazy with it.

She was hyper-aware that she'd ruined his fun trip to the seaside by bringing her self-esteem issues along for the ride. No wonder she'd been single for so long. She had no idea how to handle herself in these sorts of situations.

Finally they swung into the long driveway of the farm-house and Connor jerked the car to a halt, jamming on the handbrake and unfastening his seatbelt in one swift movement.

He turned to face her, his gaze steady and cool, but she could have sworn she glimpsed a flash of confusion in his eyes.

'Home safe,' he said.

Without another word he swung himself out of the car and strode away, letting himself in through the heavy oak door of the house.

She sat in stultified silence, staring after him, reluctantly acknowledging the throb of longing deep inside her.

He truly was the most fascinating man she'd ever met—not to mention the most devastatingly attractive. After everything he'd gone through he was still moving on with his life, making things better and infinitely more comfortable for people who had no way of achieving that by themselves. Was she *really* going to give up the opportunity to spend more time with him so easily? She'd be a total fool to end things like this.

Her heart thumped against her chest. Her body was a mess of emotions. That wasn't what she wanted. When she'd given in last night she'd told herself it was purely for the sex. A physical thing. She was going about this fling in completely the wrong way, pushing him too hard with questions he didn't want to answer and attaching emotions to things she had no business getting involved in.

And now she was overthinking things, as usual.

Keep it simple, stupid.

Jumping out of the car, she hurried after him, determined to pull things back.

Connor felt like punching the wall. What the hell was he doing, opening up about his past? For years he'd locked the memories safely in the back of his head and avoided conversations about his family with anyone he met. But Josie was different. The problem was she already knew part of the story, and he was sure she wouldn't have dropped the subject until she'd got her answers. She was a wily one.

It had seemed the simplest thing at the time to tell her everything and then move on, but in recounting the story out loud he'd brought back the paralysing feelings of insecurity and rejection he'd been repressing for years.

Her reaction had unsettled him—the comment about him being stubborn had made him feel petty and ignorant. After such a long time it seemed completely natural for him to avoid any contact with Abi, but perhaps she *had* changed? He certainly didn't recognise his sister from Josie's descriptions of her.

Her about-face on the fling had him rattled too. It was always *him* that decided when a relationship was over and he didn't like having the power taken away from him.

Not that he should care in the slightest. Josie Marchpane was nothing to him—just a blip on his radar, soon to be history.

So what was this sinking feeling in his gut?

The snug was cool and dim after the hot glare of the sun and it soothed his overheated body to sit alone in the darkness, away from Josie's tormenting presence. Maybe he should leave? It was going to be awkward as hell to stay here with her in the house—especially now she'd started mining away at his emotional barriers.

But why the hell should *he* be the one to go? The whole purpose of coming here had been to get back to base and attempt to work out why the satisfaction he'd previously reaped from his projects was eluding him now. With a start he realised he'd barely thought about that since meeting Josie.

He pondered it all now.

It wasn't as though he was bored; he had so much going on and regularly met new and interesting people. His lifestyle allowed him to keep things light and entertaining, to walk away when he felt he'd experienced all he wanted to out of a situation. It comforted him to know he could up and leave when it suited him—he enjoyed being a shadow, a ghost that left an impression but nothing tangible.

The idea of being responsible long-term for someone else chilled his blood; he was more well suited to giving little and often, spreading out the help he could offer to strangers.

Like last night. He'd enjoyed seeing Josie bloom beneath his hands—it had excited him as nothing else had in a long while—but now she knew more of him than he'd usually give up and it had left him vulnerable and uncomfortable.

He sighed, rubbing a hand over his face. Maybe he'd made a mistake, getting involved with Josie—even on a superficial level. He'd assumed she was aloof and controlled enough to handle a short fling, but apparently he'd been wrong. And she was too distracting, with her idiosyncrasies and her unnerving ability to keep taking him by surprise.

He sat up straighter in his seat.

Or perhaps this had all been part of a cunning ruse to get rid of him. He couldn't stop a smile from spreading across his face at the thought. He wouldn't put it past her.

But he didn't really believe that. Her body language gave her away; she still wanted him for real, just as he wanted her—he'd bet his Triumph on it.

He heard the front door open and close and braced himself for seeing her again.

The room dimmed even more as she stood in the doorway, blocking out the light from the hallway.

'Don't worry, I'll leave,' he said, pre-empting her opening gambit. 'Dibs wins after all.'

'Don't go.' Her voice was firm, but affable.

He frowned, surprised by her sudden change of mood.

'I'm sorry for asking so many questions,' she said, moving into the room and sitting down on the couch next to him. 'It's really not my place to judge you. Can we forget about it and enjoy the rest of our time together?' She turned to look at him. 'I promise—no work and no more questions about your past.'

The tightness eased in his chest. She was offering him a 'Get Out of Jail Free' card, but something still tugged at his conscience.

'I don't know, Josie. It's probably better if I go. It's all got a bit serious and that's definitely not what I was after. You neither, I suspect.'

Her expression hardened. 'You think I can't do this without falling for you?'

He just raised an eyebrow at her.

'I have no problem with only using you for sex,' she

said, a seductive smile lighting up her eyes, causing the hairs to stand up on his arms. 'I think we should suspend real life from this point until one of us leaves and do all the things we've both been fantasising about for the past couple of days.'

Images of what he'd like to do to her raced through his head and he had to shift in his seat to ease the sudden pressing concern at the front of his trousers.

'We need to get it out of our systems,' she went on, leaning in so close he could smell the tang of sea salt in her hair. 'Purge all that built-up sexual tension and have ourselves a sex banquet.'

Her smile was so provocative he couldn't help but smirk back.

He was already lost—even before she shifted to straddle his legs, her crotch making contact with his rock-hard erection. The hot kisses she trailed across his cheeks and nose were a light relief compared to the straining pressure in his lap. Putting his hands up to feel the heavy weight of her breasts, he heard her moan and felt her breath feather across the skin of his cheek. The heat lingered for seconds after she'd moved on to kiss the groove between his jaw and his neck.

Taking one of his wrists in each hand, she pushed his arms back, trapping them against the sofa, whilst rocking her hips against him, levering herself up at the top of each movement to catch the sensitive tip of him with the hot softness between her legs. Desperation to rip their clothes away and feel her slippery heat with his hands clawed at him, but she wanted the control here and he was totally fine with that—as long as she didn't stop goddamn moving.

Just as the thought hit him she moved down his lap, breaking contact where he needed it most, and he almost growled in frustration. Looking up at her, he saw the corner of her mouth twitch in amusement. She knew exactly what she was doing to him. He had a feeling she was paying him back for his anger and disinterest earlier.

She released his wrists so she could grasp the hem of his T-shirt and slide it up his body, the cool backs of her fingers leaving searing lines of sensation on the hot skin of his chest. Leaning forward, he allowed her to pull it over his head, feeling the soft leather of the couch stick to his heated bare skin as he leant back.

Slipping her knees between his legs, she pushed them open so she could slide her body to the floor and kneel in front of him, bringing her hot mouth down to the highly sensitised nub of his nipple. The first, semi-painful graze of her teeth made him jump in shock, before sending currents of pleasure through his body.

After the chafing bite she used her tongue to lick away the pain, before greedily sucking down on his nipple, swirling her tongue around the now erect peak. Her fingers worked the other side, as she alternately sucked and pinched, making him crazy with the dual sensation. This was punishment, all right.

His neglected erection gave a throb as she moved her free hand down the quivering flank of his chest, skirting over the dip of his belly button to find the button of his shorts. She made quick work of popping it open and yanking down his fly, pulling the stiff material away so that all was left was the thin cotton barrier of his boxers. Abandoning his aching nipples, she moved lower, using both hands to pull his trousers and underwear down his legs, then held his gaze as she brought her mouth back down to his exposed erection.

At the first flick of her tongue he nearly lost it, and a groan escaped from deep in his throat.

Any remaining resolve to leave tore out of his head as her mouth covered the tip of him, then slowly slid down, taking him inch by excruciating inch into the furnace of her mouth.

Her cool fingers traced the concavities between the muscles of his thighs, teasing their way higher, until she cupped his crown jewels in one hand and pressed a finger right below them, catching the small knot of nerves there with the pad of her finger and sending his body's euphoric response into overdrive.

'Holy hell, Josie,' he gasped, grasping his hands together behind his head and giving in totally to the pleasure of the moment as she worked her magic.

The torpid air of the snug was chilled compared to the heat that built between his thighs. Shocks of powerful sensation mirrored the still throbbing ache in his nipples as she moved her mouth up and down his shaft, flicking her tongue over the end of him at the apex of each move, drawing him right out of his own head.

How could he even have considered leaving when such sensational sex with Josie was on offer?

Her movements increased in speed, her other hand grasping the rigid base of him as she worked him over. A deep, primal urge to be inside her had him totally captive. He would have done anything for her right then, just to be allowed to reach his ecstatic peak. *Anything.*

And then he was there. Riding wave after exquisite wave of pleasure, his body jerking—out of control—before finally plummeting back down to earth again.

It was a few seconds before he felt able to open his eyes and check she was okay.

'You're an amazing woman, Josie Marchpane,' he groaned, still riding the glorious aftershocks of his orgasm.

The beatific smile she gave him when she looked up made his heart turn over. The breath rasped in his throat and his pulse raged in his veins as the blurring alarm of his reaction hit home. It was just a heat of the moment thing, he reassured himself. A crazy, abnormal response to the intensity of his climax.

Reaching down, he put his hands under her armpits and lifted her up, flipping her onto her back on the sofa and climbing over her.

He needed a way to eradicate the disturbing panicky feeling that was rising like a geyser in his chest again.

Unpopping the button of her shorts, he pulled them away, then yanked her knickers down her legs.

'Your turn,' he said, before lowering his mouth to her, obliterating everything but the sweetly aromatic smell of her skin and the intoxicating taste of her arousal.

Afterwards they took a long bath together in the claw-footed tub.

They left the windows open and the late-afternoon sun bounced off the surface of the water, reflecting shards of light against the tiled walls.

Josie swished the water in front of her, sending ripples right down to where her toes poked up through the surface. Even now she was sitting in front of him her feet stopped well short of his.

It was so peaceful she experienced a pang of pre-emptive holiday sickness. At least that was what she thought it was. She'd never had this particular feeling before. Normally she was too intent on getting back to work to feel anything but relief at returning home. But the rush and hustle of the city felt a million miles away from them right at that moment.

He'd been right about her needing distraction. The twitchiness she'd been living with for so long was greatly reduced when he was around. This was exactly what she needed.

Space. Time. Calm. A hot man and plenty of no-strings sex.

CHAPTER EIGHT

THEY SPENT THE next day in and out of bed, both hungry for more as they continued to explore each other's bodies.

They'd come to a wordless agreement to keep things only about the sex, taking care to skirt around anything personal or vaguely emotionally inflammatory. After the intensity of the past few days Josie found it a welcome relief. This kind of arrangement should have felt sordid, but Connor's easy nonchalance made it easy to bat away any niggles of apprehension. They both wanted the same thing and that made for the perfect balance in their non-relationship.

That night Connor tried to teach her how to make the dish he'd served the first time they'd eaten together, but they didn't get very far before things escalated into a food fight and they ended up having messy sex on the kitchen floor.

She hadn't laughed so much in her entire life.

This free love thing was a welcome antidote to the stress and rapidity of real life. She was a different person with Connor—someone who laughed and played around and woke up with a smile on her face instead of a frown. There was no urge to constantly compete and improve, and the surges of panic and anger that she'd lived with for as long as she could remember barely touched her consciousness.

She finally got why sex was so damn popular, having spent years feeling ho-hum about it. It was especially diverting when you had someone as moreish as Connor on tap.

Josie was in the kitchen washing up the breakfast things when Connor strode in and pressed himself close into her back, wrapping his arms around her waist and kissing the side of her neck.

'I just heard from one of the other project leaders. There's been a delay in getting materials out there so they don't need me for at least another week,' he murmured against her skin, his breath tickling the fine hairs there and sending sparks of longing straight to the erogenous zones he always made come alive when he touched her.

'Oh, okay.' She feigned nonchalance while all the while her heart sang with joy in her chest, beating out a happy rhythm.

He gave her one last sucking kiss on her neck before releasing her and leaving the room, his heavy footsteps sounding a happy pattern on the wooden floor.

She was glad he hadn't asked whether she minded, because there was no way she'd have been able to lie well enough to convince him that she didn't care whether he left or not.

A couple of days later they drove into Aix and wandered around the street markets, passing brightly canopied stalls groaning under the weight of gargantuan-sized fruit and vegetables. Josie's mouth watered as the sweetly aromatic smell of produce ripening in the sun hit her nostrils.

Stopping to point out his selection to a stallholder,

Connor chatted away in rapid French, making the guy chuckle so much he slipped them a free handful of strawberries. Josie marvelled at Connor's ability to find common ground with everyone he met, tossing a compliment here and an interested question there, drawing everyone in to the warmth of his company. She envied his people skills—they were something she knew she'd do well to study and replicate.

The alien sense of belonging left her dumbstruck as he included her in the conversation, turning his body to encompass her in his personal space and directing every other comment in her direction. They could have been a couple out for a leisurely afternoon amble around the city for all anyone else knew. A twinge of gloom came out of nowhere, pinching her chest and leaving her breathless as it hit home how false this all was. How fleeting.

She must have made some sort of gasping sound, because Connor shot her a look of concern.

'You all right, Josie?'

She nodded, flapping away his concern while scrambling to re-establish the sanguine mood she'd been so captivated by only a minute ago. It was like tipping over from being fun drunk to having had one drink too many.

'Fine, I just need to sit down and have a break. It's pretty hot out here.'

Connor took in Josie's flushed face and the deep pinch of a frown on her forehead and realised it was time to move on. The last thing he wanted was for her to collapse in the heat again. Nodding a goodbye to the stallholder, he took her arm and guided her to the side of the busy street, searching around for somewhere to sit down.

'Do you want to get a cold drink?' he asked as she

lifted the hair away from the back of her neck and flapped her hand up and down to create a wave of cool.

'Actually, I'm gasping for a coffee and something to eat,' she said, her eyes wide and troubled. 'I think my blood sugar's a bit low.'

He nodded and pointed to a small side street. 'Let's cut through here and find somewhere a bit quieter.'

He still had hold of her arm, but he didn't feel like letting it go, so he looped his wrist through the curve of her elbow, keeping her close, but still free to move easily. It comforted him to hold her near him.

The end of the street opened out onto a small square with a long strip of sandy-coloured gravel running to one side, where a group of men were playing pétanque. They paused for a minute to watch the game, and the men shouting and joshing each other as their balls landed miles from where they'd intended.

The convivial atmosphere heartened him. He was exactly where he wanted to be right now, which was a new experience. Usually he was eager to move on quickly to the next place and begin something new, always thinking ahead, not giving himself time to fully experience the moment he was in. The weight of duty he normally carried around had lifted for the time being; it was doing him good to slow down for a while.

His train of thought ground to a halt as a small hand landed on Josie's shoulder, making her jump and tug sharply on his arm.

'Excuse me, do I know you?' an English voice asked.

They both turned to face a short, middle-aged woman with a badly sunburned face and a voluminous chest spilling over the top of her ill-fitting vest. Connor could tell by Josie's expression that she was building herself up for the usual polite conversation about her sister and his hands twitched uncomfortably in sympathy. He should find a way to get them out of there quickly; he didn't want some ignorant tourist ruining what was turning out to be a pleasant outing.

The woman wrinkled her nose as she scrutinised Josie, her beady eyes raking her face.

'No, sorry, we've never met,' Josie said patiently, clearly hoping the woman would fail to make the connection and walk away.

'You look so familiar…' the woman said slowly, her brow creased in confusion.

Josie flashed her a polite smile and went to turn away just as the woman's eyes sparked with life and her brain caught up with her mouth.

'I've got it! You look just like Maddie Marchpane from *Sensational Science*—except not quite as…' She wrinkled her nose again disdainfully and wiggled her fingers in Josie's face, eager to bestow her insensitive pearls of wisdom.

Connor took an instinctive step forward, anger flaring in his chest at her witlessness, aware that the look he was giving her was less than friendly. The woman's gaze flicked to him and she stopped short, flapping a hand in front of her own face now, clearly backtracking on whichever tactless adjective she'd almost let slip.

Her face flushed red with embarrassment. 'Um… not quite as blonde.' She gave them a quavering smile. 'I'm a huge fan of Maddie—her show is wonderful,' she rushed on.

'I'll let her know you said so,' Josie said kindly. 'My sister's always delighted to hear it when people enjoy the programme.'

The woman gave her a beaming smile in return, relief that she hadn't offended Josie clear on her face. 'How nice to have a famous sister. And one as popular as Maddie too.'

'Have a great holiday,' Josie said firmly, moving away and pulling on Connor's arm to suggest he come with her.

They'd walked to the end of the square before he trusted himself to speak, the irritation still bubbling like acid in his veins. 'You're one classy lady, Josie Marchpane.'

She looked at him and laughed out loud. 'I thought she was going to pee her pants when you shot her that intimidating glare of yours.'

'Well, maybe that'll teach her to keep her pedestrian opinions to herself in the future,' he said, scowling at the woman's retreating back.

'Have you ever thought of hiring yourself out as a bodyguard? You'd make a fortune just by glowering at people.'

He snorted in response. Usually he didn't get involved in other people's conflicts, but he didn't seem to be able to stop himself when it came to Josie. She brought out the warrior in him.

They passed by a small café with tables lined up on a raised terrace, the red checked tablecloths and vases of vivacious sunflowers cheerfully gaudy against the subtle sandy gold of the stone buildings surrounding them.

'That looks like a good place. Fancy it?' he asked, nodding behind them to an empty table.

'Sure,' she said, turning and heading back to where he'd pointed.

They made themselves comfortable and a waiter brought them menus and a basket of bread.

'Hmm, there's some peculiar-sounding meals here,' Josie said, scanning the specials list she'd been handed.

'You should try something new. You never know—

you might find you like it,' he said, throwing her a challenging smile.

'You're not going to try talking me into eating snails for a laugh, are you?' she asked with a shiver, her eyes alive with mirth and her lips quirking into a bewitching grin.

He leant forward in his chair, locking his gaze with hers and tipping his head in an attempt to convey being conspiratorial. 'I don't think we need to be feeding you an aphrodisiac right now, Josie. Delicate parts of us might fall off if you get any hornier.'

She raised a defiant eyebrow. 'I seem to remember *you* jumping on *me* in the shower this morning. *And* forcing me to abandon our game of chess last night for a quickie on the floor of the snug.'

His pulse raced at the memory. He shrugged, his grin widening at her playful expression. 'I was running interference. I knew I was going to lose so I thought I'd make the game a bit more interesting.'

'You big fat cheat,' she said, kicking him gently under the table. 'Although, to give you your due, what we ended up doing after abandoning the chess game *was* much more fun.'

Gazing at her, with the hazy afternoon sunlight on her face, he thought she'd never looked so beautiful. If he'd found her impressive before it was nothing to the way he reacted to her now. She was definitely a grower; the more he was around her the more she drew him into her web of temptation.

The low pulse of arousal he experienced whenever she was near intensified exponentially. At this rate they wouldn't make it back to the farmhouse before he felt compelled to jump on her. Alfresco sex wasn't normally his bag, but he felt sure he could overlook that fact just this once.

Why couldn't life always be like this?

The question came out of nowhere, slamming him in the chest with the force of a bullet.

He needed to pull himself together. The stupefying heat and relaxed atmosphere were tricking his senses into believing this was all real, but he knew the truth. It was temporary, just like all holidays away from the humdrum of normal life. *She* was temporary, and he needed to keep a handle on that or he was going to find himself in big trouble.

The following day Connor left the farmhouse and went to the bank to handle some business transactions, leaving Josie alone for the first time in days. She'd assumed she'd be pleased to have some time on her own, but after only an hour without him she was aching for him to come back and found herself pacing the house, a nervy energy keeping her on the move between kitchen and snug, bathroom and bedroom.

In each room she delighted in the cosy comfort she'd come to know and love. A warm blush travelled across her cheeks as she realised there wasn't a room they hadn't had sex in—even the junk room hadn't been left out after she'd discovered him in there looking for a book he'd packed away and one thing had led to another.

It was already hard to think about leaving all this behind. Had it really only been two weeks? It felt as if she'd been here for months and the days and nights had merged into each other.

Despite her promise to herself to treat their affair as what it was—a fun holiday fling—she couldn't stop herself from wondering what it would be like to have Connor as a partner.

He excited and challenged her, opened her mind to things she'd spent her life hiding from, and she'd never known such peace as when she was with him. She felt so protected. As if she could leave it up to someone else to look out for her for a change.

Before she'd met Connor an incident like the one with the woman yesterday would have stayed with her for days, eating away at her fragile confidence, feeding her sense of failure and driving her to work harder, longer, faster. But not now.

His presence galvanised her, inspiring in her a poised indifference she'd never known she had. The realisation that she was learning by his example hit her like a jack-hammer. Her confidence was emerging bit by bit from the dark vault of her mind and it was Connor she had to thank for pointing the way out.

Over the past few days she'd allowed her overactive imagination to flit around the idea that he'd changed his mind about only treating this as a fling—that she'd somehow penetrated that wall of detachment he protected himself with. But surely she was kidding herself. There was no way Connor wanted more from her than a casual holiday affair. How could he? He was a drifter who didn't seem to stick anywhere for long. She needed stability in her life. Her time here had been a roller coaster, but she couldn't live like that.

Later that evening, after dinner, they snuggled up on the sofa drinking a peaty-smelling whisky that Connor had unearthed from the sideboard.

'Do you spend any time in London?' she asked tentatively.

Connor was sitting behind her, holding her against him, so she couldn't see his face, but she felt him stiffen.

'No. I hate the place. I've no plans ever to go back to England.'

She wasn't surprised. She couldn't picture him there somehow, with his casual manner and self-contained attitude. He was too big for the place—too vibrant and healthy. She knew how London could suck the life out of a person, and she couldn't bear the thought of that happening to Connor.

'So what's next for you?' she asked.

'This new project in India, then who knows?'

'It sounds like a hard life. Don't you crave some stability?' She hoped he couldn't feel the heavy thumping of her heart against his chest.

Connor snorted. 'I like things the way they are. I feel trapped if I stay somewhere too long.'

A heavy weight thunked into her stomach. 'Right.'

She thought about her own life. How different they were. Apart from the odd business trip she spent the majority of her time in one place; he never seemed to stay still for long.

'You must find it hard to hold down any relationship if you're always moving on?' She prayed the shake in her voice wouldn't give her away.

Connor nodded. 'Yeah.'

Josie waited for him to elaborate. The silence stretched on.

She wasn't ever going to see him again. She knew that. She just didn't want to believe it. He was right; they lived in different worlds. Different universes.

How was she going to go back to her old life, knowing he was out there somewhere but that she'd never see him again? What if it always felt as if a piece of her was constantly missing?

She liked him. She really, *really* liked him.

Trying to shake off the thought, she told herself she'd forget all about him once she got her head back into work, but she was uncomfortably aware that the lure of working didn't hold the appeal it once had.

What had she done? She'd gone and replaced one obsession with another, and this new one was going to stride out of the door some time very soon and never look back.

Connor cursed himself. He'd known this would happen. The subtle questions about what he was doing next and the not so subtle one asking how he could live like that were already being wheeled out. How could he have thought it was going to be any different with Josie? She'd seemed so autonomous he'd thought he'd get away with it this time, but she was already ringing conversational warning bells.

Damn it.

Not that the thought of what it would be like to see more of her hadn't flitted through his mind. But that was all it had been—a passing whim. He'd banished the thought as soon as it sprang into his consciousness. He'd promised himself he wouldn't do this again. Not after the mess with Katherine. He wasn't ready to give enough of himself to a relationship—not when there was still so much to fix in the world.

There was that hot, panicky feeling again—which he refused to acknowledge this time. It wasn't going to get the better of him. *She* wouldn't get the better of him. This thing between them had a use-by date, which was now uncomfortably close. She obviously felt it too if she was starting to ask the *Where are we going now?* questions.

A sudden blinding anger coursed through him. Why the hell was she going there when they'd agreed not to? Now he was going to look like the bad guy again when he put an end to this fling.

She turned on the sofa to face him and he had to grit his teeth and force a smile, so as not to alert her to the raging fury he was battling with.

He obviously wasn't doing a very good job because she frowned and drew back.

Before she could ask him anything else he put his hands on either side of her face and pulled her roughly towards him. Kissing her hard, he pushed her down onto her back and ran his hands up under her skirt.

He wanted to stop her asking any more of him than he felt able to give, and this was the best way he knew. As good an avoidance technique as any.

Pulling her lacy knickers roughly away from her body, he heard the delicate material rip. Opening his eyes, he saw she had hers open too and was staring at him in surprise. Tamping down on a twist of self-reproach, he moved away from her, pulling her with him and guiding her off the sofa onto her knees, so she had her back to him and her belly pressed into the soft cushions.

'Spread your legs,' he said, and she complied without a word.

Her total submission thrilled him and his erection pressed hard against the material of his trousers, eager for action. Reaching into his back pocket, he extracted a condom, then freed himself from his clothing so he could roll it on.

Shifting her skirt, he slid between her legs, pressing against her soft folds so she could feel how hard he was.

She gasped as he rubbed himself against her, the action becoming easier as she became slipperier with her own silky arousal. He nudged her clitoris each time he thrust against her and she let out a low moan as he drew back and forth over her sensitive nerves.

Hands splayed in front of her, she dropped her forehead to the cushions, refusing to look back at him. She was giving herself to him without barriers—without any kind of fight for once—and it almost stopped him in his tracks. This wasn't what he wanted. He didn't want her compliant and withdrawn. He wanted her fiery and passionate and playful.

'Just do it. Stop torturing me and *do* it.'

Her voice was ragged, strained and urgent. Even though he knew this wasn't just about the sex it didn't stop him from burying himself inside her, plunging himself right up to the hilt. Grabbing her hips in his hands, he took long, deep strokes inside her, punishing her for the words, the questions, the need.

A surge of dull pain in his chest and an aching tightness in his lungs distracted him for a second, but he battled against it. He wouldn't let it win—wouldn't let *her* win. Not this battle.

He slammed into her over and over again, hearing her grunt and gasp under him, her long hair flying across her back as they moved forcefully together. Reaching round, he found the slick nub of her clit and flicked his thumb over it, feeling her twitch and spasm beneath him as her gasps became louder and more intense.

'Come for me now, Josie,' he demanded, and she did, her tight muscles clamping around him, drawing him in deeper, the rock of her body urging him to go harder as she came.

It only took another couple of strokes before he was

there too, pouring himself into her, the disorientating sensation muddled with his anger and desperation and confusion.

As they lay recovering, their bodies pressed closely together on the sofa, Josie was horrified to find her throat tight from trying to suppress a deep sob from escaping. Her eyes burned with unshed tears and her stomach clenched in pain.

No, no, no.

This wasn't supposed to happen. This was supposed to be fun, emotion-free sex to get her mojo back. A treat.

He'd been angry with her for asking about continuing this fling when she'd promised she wouldn't, and that had been unemotional I-don't-want-to-talk-about-this sex. A way of telling her to back off without actually saying it.

'I'm going for a shower,' she managed to mutter through a painfully constricted throat, extracting herself from Connor's heavy limbs and readjusting her skirt to at least partly cover herself.

Her movements were jerky and uncoordinated and her hands shook as she flattened her hair against her head. She didn't look at him and left the room before he had a chance to comment on how strung out she was.

By the time she'd finished showering she felt almost normal again.

Almost.

She had to pull herself together. She couldn't go back to work in a worse state than when she'd left—how could she ever explain *that* to Abi? It was bad enough that she'd had sex with her friend's brother; she definitely couldn't take her emotional distress back to impact on her already shaky relationship with the staff. This was exactly why she shouldn't have let anything develop with him.

It was time to think about leaving.

If she didn't go now she'd never make it out with her heart intact.

Going into the bedroom, she found Connor dressing in jeans and a soft black cotton T-shirt that stretched across his massive shoulders and hugged the contoured muscles of his arms. Her heart lurched at the sight. God, she was going to miss his amazing body.

'What is it?' His voice was gruff.

Josie took a breath. Why was she so nervous about saying it? She was sure it would mean nothing to him if she left. In fact he'd probably be pleased to have his solitude back.

'I have to get back to London. I can't leave Abi to handle everything any longer. She must be run ragged by now.'

Connor just looked at her, his expression unreadable. He nodded. 'Right.' His hands were clenching and un-clenching at his sides. He looked away, through the win-dow at the darkening night sky.

'You can have your house back.'

'Great.'

Ask me not to go, she begged him silently. She needed to know this had meant something to him, that she wasn't just some diversion. Not that she had any right to expect that. She'd been using him too, hadn't she?

Connor turned to face her. She stood there rigidly, not sure what to do or say next. He walked towards her and she tensed in anticipation. Stopping directly in front of her, he placed a finger under her chin and tipped it up so her gaze met his.

'Is that really why you're leaving?'

'You know it's not.'

'Then don't go.'

Connor's demand both pleased and shocked her. She looked at him in disbelief, excitement bubbling in her stomach. 'What are you asking me?'

'Stay here with me for one more week. It's my birthday next Saturday. Help me celebrate.'

Her heart sank. He only wanted a few more days. Nothing more. 'I didn't think you'd be the type to celebrate birthdays.'

'I'm not usually.'

She looked away from him, barely holding it together. 'I can't. My sister's up for a Best Presenter award that weekend and I promised to go and support her.'

She'd had no intention of actually going when Maddie had asked her—she found those things excruciating to sit through on her own, being ignored while people fawned over her sister—but after talking to Connor about her somehow seemed to matter less now. The tight ball of angst she carried round with her had shrunk to a manageable size. And it was as good an excuse as any.

Connor let his hand drop.

'Okay, well, have fun and don't let the door hit you on the ass on the way out,' he said.

There wasn't a flicker of emotion on his face.

How could he behave so flippantly about this?

Because he didn't care enough.

A surge of anger exploded in her chest. 'I live in the real world, Connor. I face things head-on, even if it's tough.'

He stared at her, his expression darkening. 'How did this conversation get turned around on me?'

She let out an exasperated sigh. 'Perhaps it's your guilty conscience making the leap?'

'Josie, go home if that's what you want.'

He sounded totally unconcerned.

The pain of his rejection burned in her chest. 'So that's

it for us? You're cutting me out of your life because I won't bend to your will? I'm just another project you've completed?'

He gave her such a condescending look she wanted to prod him hard, just to get some sort of emotional reaction. Instead she did something much worse.

'Come with me to the awards ceremony,' she blurted, her heart pounding so fast she thought she might pass out.

He looked incredulous. 'And do what?'

'I don't know.' She flapped her hands in the air in exasperation. 'Just *be*.'

'You want me to make nice with your family? Shove me under their noses to win some attention away from your sister?'

'No,' she said, gritting her teeth. But she did. She wanted that, and more. *Much* more.

He sighed and rubbed a hand forcefully back and forth through his hair. 'Then what do you want from me?'

'I don't know. Nothing.'

I want you to want to keep exploring whatever the hell this thing is between us. Come to London.

But she knew she couldn't ask that of him. He'd never do it in a million years.

He took a step backwards, shoving his hands into the pockets of his jeans. 'I can't offer long-term commitment, Josie. I'm not interested in that. It wouldn't be fair to you. I'm always on the move. That's what went wrong with my other relationships—I couldn't give them the attention they needed. Anyway, I can't be with someone who puts her job before me.'

'That's your reasoning? That your past relationships didn't work so this one won't either?'

He shrugged. 'I'm a realist.'

She snorted. 'What would *you* know about realism?

When have you ever had to stick your neck out to make a go of something? You have no idea what it's like to fight for something. You've had everything given to you on a plate. You'll never have to wake up in the morning and wonder whether you still have a business to go to. You've got so much money you can afford to give it away, so please don't lecture me about how to live my life. You do whatever the hell you want, when you want, and then just up and leave when things get too hard to handle. You're mad because I'm beating you to the punch this time.'

She could see tension working the muscles in his shoulders, and as he turned to face her his jaw was clamped in anger.

'You're right. You should go. It sounds like this relationship's walked into a brick wall.'

'I didn't think this *was* a relationship.'

He gave her a cold smile. 'It's not.'

Josie felt sick. Where had the compassionate man she'd begun to unearth gone? How could he be so callous after all they'd shared?

She fought to keep her voice under control, but the pain that his words provoked was nearly blinding her. 'I thought there was more to you than this. That the loner persona was a front. But it's not, is it? You'll always be one hundred per cent for yourself. One day you'll need to stop and face what's chasing you away. Be a man.'

She knew it was a low blow, but if he was going to play dirty so was she.

Grabbing her case, she piled her stuff into it willy-nilly and forced it shut. Tears threatened to spill out, but she held them back. There was no way she was showing Connor how much this had hurt her.

He stood with his back to her, looking out of the window. He didn't say a thing.

Humiliation crashed in on her. She meant nothing to him. Less than nothing.

Dragging the case out to the front of the house, she slammed the door behind her and flopped down on the front step, staring fiercely out across the gold and purple fields that surrounded her. Their association with Connor now marred what should have been a beautiful sight.

On autopilot, she called the hotel next to the airport and booked a room, then got herself onto the next flight out to London in the morning. She completed each step without emotion, refusing to let herself acknowledge the heavy drag of sadness in her limbs.

Ten minutes later the door to the farmhouse was still resolutely shut. He wasn't coming out to stop her. He'd never change his mind.

It was time to go home.

After Josie drove away Connor sat brooding in the kitchen.

He was furious—angrier than he ever remembered being in his life. Who did she think she was, barging into his life and making judgements on him? They barely knew each other, yet she'd managed to pull him apart with just a few choice words.

He shouldn't have asked her to stay.

He wasn't sure why he had.

She'd got under his skin, that was why.

This realisation made him even more furious with her and, more crucially, with himself. He hated how out of control he felt, how panicky; it was something he tried to avoid at all costs. It was a slippery slope.

Once he gave himself to something he found it very difficult to give it up. Like his travelling. It had become part of him now, and the thought of being stationed somewhere for any length of time made him uncomfortable.

This restlessness was in his blood. He couldn't let Josie get the same hold on him. Once there, she would be there forever, haunting him.

To his utter frustration he could still smell her on him, taste her in his mouth, feel her under his fingertips. He hadn't been ready to say goodbye to her so soon and he felt jarred and uneasy.

On reflection, it was probably a good thing she was gone. It was time he went too. He'd already extended his stay here far longer than he'd planned. He needed to get back to the project, back where life was simple and free from emotional complications, or he would regret it—and God knew he didn't need any more regrets.

CHAPTER NINE

LONDON WAS SUCH a crazy, intense whirl of noise and lights after the peace of the French countryside that Josie's head throbbed when she finally made it home to Greenwich.

Walking into her apartment was like stepping back into the past. The air was stale and fusty from being sealed inside for the past couple of weeks and the atmosphere was cold and soulless compared to the warm comfort of the farmhouse.

She spent a while wandering around it in a spaced-out state, mentally changing the furniture and the decor so it would feel more homely. She needed to put some pictures on the walls and introduce a bit of colour to the place. Focusing on something simple like that helped distract her racing thoughts from what she'd left behind in France, at least in the short term.

It occurred to her that she spent so little time at home her surroundings had never really intruded on her consciousness before. They were just the background to her life. Now they seemed more important than that. She needed to be reflected in her own home. There was nothing there at the moment that was intrinsically 'her.' The place had no personality.

Was that what had happened to her? she wondered

with a shock. Was she actually as bland as her apartment? The thought terrified her. Perhaps that was why Connor had seemed so comfortable with letting her go. She'd just been a warm body in the right place at the right time for him.

The muscles in her throat squeezed so hard as she tried to stop the tears that it actually hurt. Flopping down onto the sofa, she put her head in her hands and tried to will her locked jaw to relax.

At least that proved she'd been right to go. She couldn't allow herself to care about someone who treated her with such easy indifference.

Pulling her knees up to her chin, she wrapped her arms around her legs, curling herself into a tight ball. She shouldn't have let herself get sucked into the excitement of a crazy fling, she knew that now, but it had been like a dream. It was as if someone else had taken her over, making her do things she would never usually do.

Worst. Mistake. Ever.

But she was damned if she was going to regret it. It had happened and it was best to fold it away into the cupboard of her mind and move on.

The most frustrating thing was that she was in much better shape to make a relationship work now she'd made some life-changing decisions about how to fix what had gone wrong before. She'd been floundering before she'd met Connor, focusing on the wrong things entirely and missing out on the simple joys of life—like laughing and cooking and playing and having spectacular sex. He'd brought the happiness back into her life for a few tantalising days, then shut the door in her face.

Suddenly the thought of forgetting Connor was too much to deal with, so she got up and distracted herself by playing her piano, hammering away on the keys with her headphones plugged into the keyboard so as not to disturb the neighbours until all the passion and angst drained out of her.

The following morning Josie woke up groggy from too little sleep. Her head had spun with thoughts of Connor and what might have been until the early hours, making her twitchy and tense, until she'd finally dropped off into a troubled sleep just as the sun made an appearance through the chink in her curtains.

Dragging herself out of bed, she had a speedy shower and dressed in one of her work suits.

Shrugging on her jacket, she took one last fleeting look in the mirror.

Not good.

Her eyes were puffy, as if she hadn't slept for a week, and her skin looked sallow beneath her tan.

So this is what unhappiness looks like.

There was a subdued atmosphere hanging amongst the smattering of colleagues who were already diligently working away at their desks when she arrived at work.

A few people glanced up as she passed them, the expressions on their faces ranging from wary to downright hostile. Jeez, she had a lot of making up to do here.

Abigail was already sitting at her desk, madly typing away on her computer. Josie couldn't help but marvel at how different she was from her brother. Abi only came up to her chin when standing, making her just over five foot tall, and her dark hair and eyes were in total contrast to Connor's blond, blue-eyed appeal. There was a trace of family resemblance around their eyes, though, and as Abigail looked up and smiled at her Josie felt a pang of horror as she recognised Connor's grin.

She hadn't bargained on feeling like this around Abi. She'd been so focused on getting back to work it hadn't occurred to her how she'd deal with being around Connor's sister. She would have a daily reminder of him now.

Her discomfort must have shown in her face, because Abigail frowned.

'God, Josie, you look terrible. I thought a holiday would have done you some good, not made you more tired.'

'I just didn't sleep well last night, that's all.' She brushed off Abi's concern, desperate to focus on what needed to be said here and to forget all about the reason for her restless night.

Abi continued to look at her for a moment, before gesturing for her to sit down on the leather sofa in the corner with her. 'You want some coffee? You look like you could do with some.'

'No, I'm okay, thanks.'

'Did you actually manage to get some rest while you were away?'

Judging by Abi's expression, she clearly thought Josie had been working and angsting about the business the whole time she was in France. Going by her rough appearance that morning, it was a reasonable assessment.

'I did. After the first couple of days I didn't do any work at all.'

At least she didn't have to lie about that. Unfortunately the memories of what she *had* done threatened to trounce her composure before she'd had a chance to apologise for her crazy behaviour.

Abi raised her eyebrows but didn't say anything.

Sitting up straighter, Josie folded her hands in her lap, her heart thumping in her chest. Apologising to Abi was going to be more nerve-racking than she'd anticipated.

Her palms were sweaty as she primed herself to say the words she needed to get out, pushing any qualms out of her mind.

'I'm so sorry for all the problems I've caused recently. I've been selfish, expecting everyone to fall in line with what I want and losing my temper when they didn't. So childish.' She shook her head and gave Abi a sheepish look.

The relief on Abi's face provided the first shot of happiness she'd experienced since leaving the farmhouse.

'I've been working too much, and it's affected my judgment,' Josie said, leaning forward in her seat. 'But my head's on straight now and I'm ready to get back to it without losing my temper—or my mind—again.'

'That's great to hear.'

'And I'm going to apologise to the rest of the staff in a minute. I want them to feel they can approach me with any problems and that I won't bite off their heads and spit them out.'

Abi chuckled. 'You *can* be a bit fierce sometimes.'

Josie sighed. 'Yeah.' She squirmed inside as she remembered how stern she'd been with Connor when he'd first shown up. And how little it had affected him.

'Well, I'm glad a holiday helped.'

Before she could check herself Josie blurted, 'I met Connor at the farmhouse.'

Abigail became very still.

'He arrived a few days into my holiday and needed somewhere to stay.'

Abi turned to look at her, her dark eyes roving Josie's face. 'I'm sorry. His lawyers said he was in South America.' Her voice wobbled a little and her eyes flicked down to her lap. 'How is he?'

Josie regretted her insensitivity. The mention of Connor's name clearly had Abi rattled.

'He's fine,' she said, careful to keep any emotion out of her voice.

Stubborn and emotionally stunted, but physically fine was what she really wanted to say. In fact he was more than fine. Her skin warmed at the memory of his strong body holding her close. A blush crept up her neck and she willed it not to reach her face and give her away.

'What happened? Did he let you stay?' Abi asked, obviously fighting to keep her cool in the face of the unexpected bombshell.

'Yeah, after a bit of negotiation. He's a tough cookie, your brother.'

'Tell me about it.' The pain in Abi's eyes confirmed exactly how she felt about him. 'Did he...say anything about me?'

'Uh...' she began tentatively.

Should she really be telling Abi this? *No* was the honest answer, but she wanted to hear Abigail's side of it. To make sense of it all. She had to know the other side of the story or it would eat away at her forever.

'He did tell me a bit about the rift between you both.'

Abigail looked at her sharply. 'What did he say?'

'Well, he was cagey about it, but he insinuated that you went back on your word to you grandma and gave your inheritance to your parents, then threatened that if he didn't do the same he'd never be welcome in the family again.' She kept her voice light, as if suggesting she didn't believe a word of it.

She so wanted to know that it hadn't happened like that. She needed to hear something negative about Connor to give her a reason to believe he wasn't as perfect as he seemed. A way to ease the torment of missing him.

Abigail sighed and dropped her head into her hands, rubbing them across her face. Finally lifting her head, she looked Josie full in the face, her eyes filled with pain. 'All totally true, I'm afraid.'

Josie was floored. She'd never expected Abigail just to own up to it in such a straightforward manner. Surely there had to be more to it than that? She waited for her friend to continue, her fingers tapping nervously on her legs.

Abi took a deep breath before answering. 'I was really jealous of his relationship with our grandmother. They got on so well and I always felt left out.'

She looked away, her gaze skirting around the room, finally returning to a spot on the floor in front of her.

'I was really unhappy as a child. Our parents didn't give us much attention and I took out my anger on the people closest to me—Connor and my grandma.' She rubbed a hand across her forehead. 'I used to try to get Connor into trouble all the time—just for some attention, I guess—and he hated me for it. Anyway, when our grandma died she left us her inheritance—gave most of it to Connor and a small amount to me. It nearly destroyed me at the time. It was proof that she loved Connor more than me and I didn't know how to handle that feeling.'

Her voice broke on the last word and she paused for a few seconds to regain her poise.

Josie put a reassuring hand on her arm, her heart sinking with wretchedness for her friend.

'Then the opportunity to help our parents came up,' Abigail continued when she'd steadied herself. 'They needed a huge cash injection to keep their business alive and suddenly I was of interest to them. I felt wanted—needed—for the first time in my life. I'm ashamed to say I gave in straight away and promised them the money. I was still furious with Connor and I tried blackmailing him into giving up his share too. He refused, and I helped my parents kick him out of the family.'

Her eyes filled with tears.

'I'm not proud of what I did. I wish I could take it back and make everything right with us again. But he's not interested in talking to me any more. I've tried so many times over the years to get him to speak to me I've lost count. But I can't really blame him for not wanting anything to do with me.' She brushed a tear angrily away from her face. 'Connor always handled things so much better than me. I was a mess. Still am, really.' She smiled sadly through her tears.

He *was* a handler, Josie realised. Clearly he'd been doing it all his life, and the thought of allowing someone else to dictate how he felt or reacted or suffered was too much for him. It was safer and easier to be alone, with only himself to manage. She could comprehend that. Not that it meant losing him hurt any less, but it helped her to be able to understand *why* she couldn't have him. It wasn't a failure in her; it was an inability to trust in him.

At least that was what she was choosing to believe.

Poor Abi. She knew exactly what it was like to be on the receiving end of Connor's disdain and it wasn't fun.

Putting out a hand, she rubbed her friend's arm gently, hoping in some way to show her she still loved her and she understood. 'I'm sorry.'

'What for?'

'For bringing it up.'

Abi gave her head a small shake and seemed to pull herself together. She let out a long sigh and smoothed her hands down her skirt, composing herself.

'It's okay. Just something I have to live with.'

Josie's frustration levels slammed into the red. It was

absolutely gutting to see the two of them divided over something that had happened so long ago.

'So, Josie, what exactly are you going to do to get the staff back on your side?' Abi asked, breaking into her thoughts and lightening the sombre atmosphere with a hopeful smile.

'I'm going to start by grovelling,' Josie said, standing up and taking a breath, determined to make *something* right. The only thing within her control.

Striding to the other end of the room, where she'd left her bag and a box that she'd brought from the bakers that morning, she pulled out a chair and stepped up onto it, turning to face the now full room.

Clearing her throat loudly, she waited until she had the full attention of the staff before beginning her apology, her hands sweaty and shaking at her sides.

'I just wanted you all to know how sorry I am for being such a bitch recently.' There was a low murmur of whispers, but she chose to ignore them and plough on before she lost her nerve. 'I'm going to try really hard from now on to be more patient and hopefully more approachable. If not, you have permission to kick my butt. Hard.'

There were a few giggles at this and she took heart at the friendly response.

'I know it's not much, but I've brought in a cake for you all to share as a token of my appreciation for all the hard work you've put in recently.'

She reached down to the table next to her and lifted the cake she'd picked up that morning, which had the word *Sorry* iced on it in large letters.

'I'm going to skulk away now, and leave you all to it, but I'll see you tomorrow,' she said, stepping down from the chair and turning to give Abi a smile. Her friend smiled back and gave her a silent clap, nodding her head in appreciation.

She was under no illusion that she was going to be totally forgiven right away, but it was a start.

Josie felt drained for the rest of the day. She paced aimlessly around London, barely taking in her surroundings.

The South Bank hummed with life as she wandered past bars filled with people out enjoying a drink in the sunshine. Their chatter and laughter rang out across the water, mixing with the hypnotic sound of the tide lapping against the shore. Josie imagined she was floating above it all, in some kind of dispossessed state. Disconnected.

The sun penetrated her clothes and warmed her skin. Vitamin D. Good for her happiness levels. Her stomach plunged as Connor's words filtered through her mind.

How was it possible to ache for someone so much?

Being with him had made her question exactly what she wanted from life. He'd drawn back the veil to show her how much fun she was missing, leaving an aching sadness in her belly for all the wasted opportunities, all the friends she'd let fall by the wayside. She was proud of what she'd helped achieve with the business but, like any addiction, she'd let it overtake her life to the point where it had become unhealthy.

Cold turkey with a side order of Connor had been a roaring success.

Connor. She'd got over her crazy workaholic attitude. Now she just needed to get over him too.

The hopelessness of the situation came back to haunt her every so often, and she had to duck into a shop or gallery in order to give her brain something else to focus on. There was a constant tight feeling in her throat and her stomach churned, so she didn't even bother to try and eat anything.

She knew what she needed to do. She needed to arrange some counselling to work through her anger issues, stop living in Maddie's shadow and be her own person—take responsibility for her actions. Make the effort to start seeing friends again, cut back on the amount she was working and get her bloody life back.

Meet someone new, perhaps?

Sadness crushed her at the thought. She didn't want anyone else. Connor was so right for her in a lot of ways.

But he didn't want her. Not for a proper relationship anyway. He'd made that very plain.

Connor had been sure he'd be able to banish the thought of Josie and leave France with a clean conscience.

But he couldn't.

He'd thought he'd be pleased to be on the move again. But he wasn't.

There hadn't been a day in the past week when he hadn't thought about her, and it was becoming a problem. He was having trouble sleeping, which was really unusual for him. When he did sleep he dreamed about Josie, and when he woke to find he wasn't holding her he felt as if someone had punched him in the gut.

He'd gone out every evening to sit by himself, nursing a beer and thinking, thinking, thinking.

A couple of brave and not unattractive women had approached him in the bars as he'd sat staring into his drinks and he'd talked to them, willing his recalcitrant brain to give them the opportunity to impress him, but he'd found them puerile and dull compared to Josie's exhilarating company.

She was one of a kind, that woman, and he'd let her slip through his fingers.

After his family's dismissal of him he'd spent so long on his own he'd forgotten how to care about someone else. Josie had reminded him of how good it could feel. The problem was she'd also highlighted how terrifying it was to trust someone with his affections again. Hence that panic attack.

He'd been searching for unconditional love from his partners—something he'd been missing since he'd lost his grandmother—but he had no right to expect that. He needed to earn it.

It occurred to him that he'd used his family's lack of interest in him over their business as a convenient excuse when he'd wanted to end a relationship, because Josie's passion about her career, her drive and determination, were the things that he valued most about her.

He spent his days in a sleep-deprived daze and started making mistakes with the project, which he couldn't afford to do.

He missed her. He missed her smile; he missed her energy and her passion. He missed the way she played music on her legs as if they were a piano, and the way she looked at him with those beautiful intelligent eyes.

He'd told himself to forget her when she'd left him in France, that there was no point pursuing anything with her. The whole gamut of arguments had run through his head. She was too wrapped up in her career to be worth the effort. He wanted her, but he didn't want it to turn into anything too serious. It wasn't fair on either of them. She was too work-focused. He was too transient. It would never work. He'd be an idiot to open the whole thing up again.

None of those arguments seemed to work. She was still all he could think about.

It was going to take a lot more than he'd first thought to get Josie Marchpane out of his head. She'd somehow instilled herself into his psyche and no matter what he thought about she wouldn't goddamn go away.

Perhaps he'd finally found a reason to stop leaving? Was Josie going to be the one who helped him find the peace he'd been craving for so long? Could he allow himself to trust that they had a future? Could she be the one to keep him grounded? There was a good chance that he could answer yes to all those questions.

Without the distraction of Josie's dynamic presence it had all come rushing in on him. The emptiness. The total singleness of his existence. She'd opened Pandora's Box in his mind and all the angst and pain had come rushing out.

Before meeting Josie he'd been fine, hopping from girlfriend to girlfriend over the years, never getting too involved, never giving too much of himself. That had been why Katherine had riled him so much—she'd been more demanding than the rest and he'd found himself plagued by her to the point of being stalked. Poor Katherine. He knew what it felt like now to want someone so much you were willing to make a fool of yourself for them.

It was time to stop running. To turn around, face his fears in an open and honest way and trust they wouldn't knock him on his ass.

CHAPTER TEN

WALKING INTO THE grand lobby of the hotel where the awards ceremony was taking place, Josie steeled herself to face her family.

Barely acknowledging the opulent surroundings and the throngs of famous faces, she pushed her way through towards the ballroom, where a stage was set up for the show.

She'd managed to duck out of the past few family get-togethers, but she knew it was time to get over her anxieties. She was just as much a part of the family as Maddie and she refused to consider herself secondary any longer. This was her getting on with her life, moving forward. She would face them and come out fighting on the other side.

Her mother was standing in the doorway to the ballroom and as soon as she spotted Josie she came busying over, resplendent in a heavily shoulder-padded eighties throwback gown and six-inch heels with diamante bows. Clearly Josie was completely underdressed in her simple slip dress and flats, if her mother's face was anything to go by.

'You made it, then?'

The condescension in her voice made Josie's pulse quicken.

Keep cool and ignore! Ignore! The words ran through her head. She'd probably need to turn it into a mantra and repeat it ad nauseum if she was going to survive a night with her mother at this thing and leave with her head held high. But she would do it. She would be serene and poised.

'Follow me. It's about to begin. We don't want to embarrass ourselves by being late to the table,' her mother said, beckoning her with a flapping hand. 'They've put us right at the front.' She moved her head back so her mouth was lined up with Josie's ear. 'I suspect we're there so Maddie can get out easily to the stage,' she said, not bothering to lower her voice a jot and wiggling her eyebrows as if she was imparting some great secret to the world.

Clearly Maddie *not* winning this thing would not be tolerated.

Josie followed her mother's swinging bottom, scooting through the packed tables, keeping her head high. She would *not* be intimidated by all the hoopla.

When they reached their destination she only managed a feeble wave at her sister and father before there was an announcement about the ceremony starting in five minutes.

Sitting down next to them, she crossed her legs and straightened her skirt, ready to take her place as 'loving sister' in front of all Maddie's friends and admirers.

'Have you been away, Josie?' her father asked, leaning in, a studious frown on his face. 'It looks like you've been out in the sun.'

She gave him a tight smile. 'Yes. I went to France for a couple of weeks.'

The look on his face didn't give her much hope that this was going to be an easy conversation.

'So who was looking after your business while you

were *holidaying*?' He said the last word as if she'd actually been in prison for drug smuggling instead of having some well-needed time out.

'Abi had it all under control.'

He nodded. 'I see.'

She thought that was it. That she'd got away without having to elucidate. But unfortunately her mother had other ideas.

'Isn't it a bad time for you to be going away, Josie?' she asked, giving her trademark concerned frown. 'If you want that business to actually make some money you should be fully focussing your energy there. Surely there's time for a break once you've managed to start making a dent in the marketplace?'

Josie wondered why her hands were hurting—until she looked down to see that she'd made deep welts in her palms with her nails. Her heart raced as adrenaline and anger surged through her.

She was not putting up with this. No way. Not any more. She was worth more than a disgruntled footnote in her parents' encyclopaedia of life.

'The business is fine,' she said through clenched teeth. 'I, on the other hand, am not. I'm tired of trying to please you. I realise now it's an impossible task, and I'm not prepared to waste any more time or energy on it. My business is just that. Mine. I'm doing it for *me* now, not you.'

She realised she was pointing a shaky finger at their shocked faces but she was too far into her rant to stop.

'I may not be famous or noteworthy, but I *am* making a difference in my own small way. And that's good enough.' She took a deep, calming breath and splayed her hands on the table, leaning in towards them and looking directly from one set of shocked eyes to another. 'It's good *enough*.'

Sitting back, she smoothed her skirt over her knees

again with shaky hands and looked over at her sister, who had seemingly missed the whole show by chatting to her neighbour at the table. Not that it mattered. This wasn't about Maddie, it was between her and her parents.

'Okay, Josie. Okay,' her father said to the side of her head.

She turned to look at him and he gave her a conciliatory nod, putting a steadying warm hand on top of hers.

Luckily she was saved from bursting into tears by a loud announcement telling them that the show was about to start and asking everyone to find their tables.

Noise levels rose too much to make conversation after that as more people hurried in to take their seats.

Straightening her spine and pulling back her shoulders, Josie regained her poise and waited calmly for the show to begin, ignoring the whispered conversation going on between her parents next to her. It didn't matter what they said now. All that mattered was that she'd said her piece and she was ready and willing to get on with her life.

But she couldn't stop herself from wishing Connor was there with her. She would have loved him to see her giving her parents what-for, and this whole horrible debacle wouldn't seem half as awful in his presence. He'd find a way to make it fun.

Her stomach plummeted to her toes and her throat contracted painfully as she imagined him there, squeezing her hand and giving her that wry grin of his.

Taking a deep breath, she forced herself to focus on the large spotlit stage until she was able to relax out of the ache of melancholy. She had to stop thinking like that; it was only going to make it harder to get over him. It was onwards and upwards from here. No looking back. No regrets.

The lights dimmed and the host of the ceremony, a rising star on the UK comedy scene, mounted the stage and greeted the audience. A hush fell over the crowd and they listened in rapt silence as he announced the first nominations.

Josie's mind wandered as short clips of the nominated shows played on a large screen above them. She wondered what Connor was doing right at that moment. Probably something exciting and worthy that would put her dull existence to shame. Her humiliating attempt to get him to come here came back to haunt her and she flushed hot with shame. She'd been so angry with him for rejecting her that she'd lost her senses. What an idiot she was. She was almost glad she was never going to see him again; she was ashamed of how ridiculous she'd been.

Realising with a start that everyone was clapping the winner of the category, she joined in a beat too late, garnering herself a stern look from her mother. Smiling sheepishly, she resolved to pay more attention to her surroundings and eject all thoughts of Connor from her head.

After all, he wasn't part of her life any more and he wasn't likely to be any time soon.

Connor stood at the back of the room as the awards ceremony rolled out on the stage in front of him. Cameras were stationed at every available angle of the grand room and the place buzzed with excited chatter. The tables where the audience sat were dark compared to the dazzling light of the stage, so he had to work hard to locate where Josie was seated with her sister and parents. He finally spotted her.

She sat, spine straight, eyes trained on the stage, a forced smile plastered onto her face as her sister's name was announced as the winner of Presenter of the Year.

Maddie gave the camera trained on her an almost comical fake surprise expression as the spotlight found her, and then she leant across to hug her mother and father before sweeping off towards the stage. Josie sat, ramrod-straight and ignored, at the other side of the table. She seemed smaller than she had in France, as if the weight of being here was pressing down on her, squashing her into a less than Josie-sized space.

A blast of possessive anger nearly knocked Connor off his feet. How could they blatantly snub her like that? His Josie. His sparky, smart, funny, fascinating Josie.

He itched to march over there and rescue her from this nauseating display of self-glorifying nonsense. She deserved better than being sidelined in the corner whilst this circus happened around her.

After her sister's win, the host called for a break and there was a sudden ruckus of chairs being scraped back and loud conversation as people got up and headed over to the winners to bestow their congratulations.

This awards ceremony had been just as awful as she'd anticipated, but Josie was still glad she'd come. She knew the only way to overcome these feelings of inadequacy around her sister was to face them head-on and walk away with her head held high. There would be no more hiding from life and no more jealousy; it was a leech she was going to burn off, no matter what it took.

Knowing she could entertain and enthral someone as incredible as Connor—even temporarily—had gone a long way to persuading her there was more to her than she'd supposed. She would celebrate all her successes from now on, even the small ones, and never, ever compare them to someone else's again. She would be the queen of her own universe.

She stood up and wandered off to the bar in the adjoining room as their table was swamped with well-wishers hoping to get a piece of her sister. Maddie already looked exhausted from all the fawning attention and having to be on her best behaviour. How could she have ever been jealous of that? It was the epitome of her worst nightmare. She needed to remember that the next time she experienced debilitating jealousy about her sister's success. Everything came with its own problems, after all—even fame and adoration.

The bar was quiet compared to the shouty hubbub of the ballroom, and she let out a long breath of relief as the silence wrapped around her, soothing her ringing ears and throbbing head.

'Hi, Josie.'

The bottom of her stomach hit the floor and all the air rushed out of her lungs at the sound of a deep, smooth voice she'd know anywhere.

Connor.

She spun round to find him standing behind her, glorious in a black shirt and dark blue jeans, his blond hair rumpled, his ice-blue eyes ringed with dark circles. If anything, he seemed larger and even more dominating than she remembered. All she could do was stand and stare at the vision in front of her, an irritating excitement building in her stomach.

'How did you find me?' she blurted. 'I mean, what are you doing here?' she corrected, trying to keep her tone neutral, but failing to keep the quaver of hopeful excitement out of her voice. He only had to look at her with those gorgeous cool blue eyes and she turned to mulch.

'Abigail told me where you'd be.'

'You've seen her?'

'I called her.'

'That's great,' she said, the pleasure and surprise at the fact she'd actually got through to him on some level momentarily overtaking the exhilaration of his appearance.

He looked at her levelly but didn't say anything. His silence unnerved her.

'Right. So, are you up for an award tonight or are you just here stalking me?' She'd meant it as a joke—a throwaway comment to distract him from the total chaos of her response to his appearance—but of course it came out sounding more serious than she intended.

'Hardly.' Connor raised a derisive eyebrow but shifted on his feet, crossing his arms in front of him.

'So what are you doing in London? Something I thought I'd never see.' This was like pulling teeth. Her throat was tight with tension and she had to fight to keep tears from welling in her eyes. She would *not* go to pieces, though. No *way*.

Connor's gaze flicked up to hers, his eyes hard behind his frown. 'Look, I don't want to leave things the way we did. I admit I was frustrated with you for leaving early and I reacted badly. I wanted to come and apologise face-to-face for the way I behaved.'

'What? You mean you're not planning on getting up on the stage to announce your apology to the whole room?' she said.

The inability to keep stupid jokes from tumbling out of her mouth was embarrassing, but not surprising considering how tense she was.

The comment earned her a smile, but it didn't quite penetrate the disquiet in his eyes.

What the hell did this mean? Was he only here to say sorry? Her heart thumped in her ribcage with alarming force.

'Okay. Well, we both said some things we shouldn't

have. Let's just forget about it,' she said quickly. She needed air. Or maybe a double shot of vodka to calm her raging nerves.

A tense silence fell between them as they looked at each other and she became aware of her fingers tapping against her legs.

Why was he still here if all he'd wanted to do was apologise? He'd done that. He should be striding out of there by now, mission accomplished.

'Why are you really here, Connor?'

He ran a hand over his eyes, his shoulders slumping a notch. 'I've been thinking about what you said.'

'About you needing to man up? I'm sorry about that.'

He put a hand up to stop her. 'The thing is, Josie, I've been on my own for so long I don't know how to care about someone else any more. I thought I wanted to be on the move because it's what I'm used to. I've been doing it since I was eighteen and I believed it was what defined me. It's not. Not really.'

'What changed your mind?' Her words came out as a whisper.

He moved towards her and touched her arm gently. 'You did. I miss being around you. Frustrating though you are sometimes. We're so different, but we totally work together.'

'Immovable object meets irresistible force?' She could barely get the words out.

He smiled. 'That's a good description of us.'

Her head spun. What was going on here? Had Connor really materialised in the middle of Maddie's awards ceremony to tell her he'd changed his mind? Or was her under-rested, overstressed brain playing tricks on her?

She needed a minute to pull herself together.

'Let's move somewhere a bit more private,' she said,

nodding towards a quiet corner where they could meld into the shadows more easily. There was no way she was having this conversation in full public view—not if she was going to end up in pieces on the floor.

Connor's stomach clenched in fear as he realised Josie wasn't responding quite the way he'd hoped. She seemed to be miles away, her eyes unfocused, as if she was thinking about something else entirely. Maybe that was her way of coping with being around him again. Or perhaps she was over him already?

The thought made his chest constrict and a slow flood of dread seeped through his veins.

No. Not possible. Not if she felt anything like the way he did.

He was quiet as he searched her face for any kind of emotion. Her eyes flickered under his scrutiny, as if she was trying to hide something from him. The silence was clearly making her nervous.

'Josie?' Connor looked at her intently, his brow furrowed. 'Don't tell me you've changed your mind about us, because I don't believe it.'

She crossed her arms against her chest and paused for a beat, seeming to gather her thoughts. Finally she looked up at him, her gaze steady. 'After I left I did some serious thinking,' she said. 'You were right. I would have had a nervous breakdown if I'd carried on the way I was going. You helped me get some perspective on life. Thank you for that.'

'Well, I'm happy to have helped.' A steady and severe pulse throbbed in his head; panic was rising in his belly. This time the potential of an attack played at the edge of his consciousness in response to the paralysing terror that she was about to tell him where he could stick his apology.

'I'm glad I met you. I needed a wake-up call,' she said.

He wasn't sure where she was going with this. His hands shook at his sides and he put them behind his back so she wouldn't see. If she was about to give him the brush-off he wanted to get out of there with as much dignity as he could muster.

'So what are you going to do about it?' He hated how breezy his voice sounded. If only she knew how he was burning up inside maybe she wouldn't prolong the agony she was putting him through.

'I'm going to slow things down a bit. Get some semblance of a life back. Talk some things through with a counsellor. Whatever I do, I'm not going to allow my work to take over my life again.'

'Okay.'

Josie looked at him steadily. 'I have to admit I was furious with you for sticking your nose into my business at first, but I realise you were only trying to help in your strange, lopsided way.'

He snorted gently. 'Yeah, well, I've been trying to save the world for so long I don't know when to stop.'

'I thought you were going to India?'

The off-subject question brought him up short. 'I did, but I handed the project to someone else to manage this time.'

It was now or never. He took a step closer to her, putting a hand on her arm in the hope that he could connect with her.

'I had to come back and see you. I never should have let you leave. I was an idiot to say no to you—to a relationship with you.' He ran a hand through his hair in agitation. 'I thought it would be best for us both to move on and forget each other, but to be honest I've been miserable without you. You're what I want. What I've been looking for for so many years. I was just too stupid to realise it.'

Josie froze, staring down at the ground. He waited for her response, trapped breath burning his lungs until he thought he couldn't stand it any longer.

'Me too,' she said finally, looking up directly into his eyes, her expression a mixture of pain and hope. 'Life's no fun without you.'

Relief flooded through him and he let out a long, low sigh. 'Thank God for that.' He moved towards her, his eyes not leaving hers, until their bodies were merely millimetres apart.

She put a hand against his chest. 'I'm not the easiest person to live with.'

'That's okay. I like difficult women,' he said, tucking a curl of hair around her ear, desperate now to feel her soft lips against his, but knowing there was more to say before that could happen.

'How are we going to make it work?' she asked, her anxiety obvious in the quaver of her voice.

'I could base myself in London…for you.'

'Really? You'd do that?'

'I'd still need to be away a lot. We're going to need determination and tenacity to keep this relationship on track.'

'I have those qualities in abundance.'

'How are you at phone sex?'

He grinned and she smirked back.

'I suck at it. But practice makes perfect.'

'And we'll have a lot of holidays away. And I mean a *lot*.'

'Okay.'

'You have to meet me halfway, Josie. I can't go through this if you're not fully with me.'

'We can make this work, I know we can.'

Finally he brought his mouth down hard on hers, his hands cupping her face. Relief surged through him. He had a flash of what lay before them: a strong, equal partnership, one that would be challenging but totally worth the effort.

She kissed him back fiercely, her fingers winding into his hair, until they were both breathless and panting.

'So you trust me not to turn back into the work-focused shrew I once was?' she said as they finally pulled apart.

He laughed. 'I trust you.'

'And you don't mind taking on the black sheep of my family?'

'I can't believe they love someone as amazing as you any less, Josie, but, no, I don't care what your family thinks.'

She gave him a sad smile. 'I've come to the conclusion that I need to accept that none of us will ever change and make peace with that.'

'Very sensible.'

'Speaking of family and sensible,' she said, looking at him coyly, 'and not meaning to break the mood or anything, but I spend a lot of time with your sister and she's a very good friend of mine. You can't keep pretending she doesn't exist.'

He rubbed a hand over his forehead, smoothing away the uneasy frown. 'I know. When I spoke to her yesterday I arranged to meet her for a drink and talk things through. You're right—it's time to move on from the past. Something I laughably thought I *had* been doing, but was actually failing miserably at.'

She smiled, and a satisfied warmth spread through him. 'I'm glad.'

'Kudos to you, by the way, for getting through my thick skull. I didn't realise how much you'd influenced me until I was picking up the phone and talking to Abi.'

She grinned. 'So the drip-drip approach worked.'

'Yeah, smarty-pants. You got me.'

'Well, you never would have made that decision if I'd nagged you to do it. You're too damn stubborn.' She slapped him gently on the arm. 'Control freak.'

'Workaholic!'

'Dromomaniac!'

He gave her a puzzled frown.

'It means you have a mania for travel.'

'Yeah, well, I'm not so maniacal about it now. Not when I have such a good reason to stay put,' he said, dropping his mouth to hers and savouring the sweetly familiar softness of her lips.

There was a commotion at the entrance to the bar and Josie reluctantly pulled away from the kiss to see a large group of people walking in, with Maddie at its epicentre.

'Let's get out of here,' she said, not wanting to have to introduce Connor to her family tonight. Nor her family to Connor, for that matter. Not until she'd had time to get her head around everything. And she really didn't want this moment to be overshadowed by her sister's overwhelming presence.

'Why don't you want me to meet Maddie?'

She sighed. How could she have thought Connor wouldn't call her on it?

There was no point in lying—not after she'd resolved to stop hiding from her fears.

'Because I'm afraid that when you look at me afterwards all you'll see is a watered-down version of her.'

He frowned. 'You think I'm going to drop you and run off with your sister?'

She shrugged. 'It's happened in the past.'

He barely had time to flash her a look of concern before Maddie caught sight of them both and swept gracefully over, her eyes zeroing in on Connor as if he were a magnet and she were a beautiful, beguiling, sister-surpassing iron missile.

'Josie, who's *this*? I didn't know you were bringing a date tonight.'

Josie's shoulders drooped, despite her determination not to let her sister's overwhelming presence intrude on her newfound and apparently rather shaky confidence. 'This is Connor. Connor—my sister, Maddie.'

Maddie gave him one of the devastating smiles that had made her such a hit with the TV-viewing public and Josie's stomach crashed to the ground. *Please, please don't let Maddie make a play for him. Not tonight. Not when things are so fresh and raw and precariously balanced.*

Connor gave her a steady smile. 'I just want to tell you what a huge fan I am.'

Maddie's grin widened, then faltered as he put his arm around Josie's shoulder.

'Of your sister,' he said, drawing Josie close to his body. 'She's the most amazing woman I've ever met and you should be proud to have her as part of your family.'

Maddie opened and shut her mouth in surprise, before pulling herself together—ever the consummate professional. 'I am.'

Josie could barely stop herself from laughing. Her sister's face was a picture. She'd never seen her so rattled.

Maddie stepped forward, blocking Connor with her back and leaning in to Josie as if giving her a sisterly hug.

'My God, he's a bit bloody gorgeous. Where have you been hiding him?' she whispered against her ear.

Drawing back, she waggled her eyebrows and smirked over at Connor. He gave her one of his indifferent smiles back.

Maddie looked ruffled at his cool response to her, but brushed it off quickly, looking over her shoulder for someone else to talk to. 'Thanks for coming to support me, Josie. I'm really pleased you're here,' she said evenly, giving her an extra hard squeeze on the arm, then gliding away to her admirers and being swallowed back into the crowd.

'Well, that was my sister,' she said, giving a small shrug of her shoulder and rocking back on her heels, testing his response.

Connor nodded thoughtfully. 'I can see why you have such an issue being related to her.'

Josie's heart plummeted. So he had been impressed by Maddie after all; he'd just done a bang-up job of disguising it.

Connor frowned at her less than enthusiastic response to his statement and pulled her in close, wrapping his arm tightly around her middle so she could feel the hardness of his muscles against her belly.

'I can honestly say you have absolutely no need to worry about me running off with your sister.'

She met his eyes and saw the sincerity in his gaze. Leaning forward, she planted a firm kiss on his mouth, attempting to convey through the osmosis of her touch that she really, truly believed him. When she drew away he was smiling at her. Apparently she'd been successful.

'It would never work with me and Maddie, anyway,' he said, leaning in to nuzzle the flashpoint on her neck that, when kissed, always made her lose her mind.

'What makes you say that?' She struggled to get the words out.

'Because if my ego and her ego ever got together I think the world would probably implode.'

She giggled in response, happiness making her light-headed.

Pulling back, he kissed first her cheeks, then her nose, his breath feathering over her skin.

'You know I wouldn't change a thing about you,' he said, firmly kissing one side of her mouth and then the other. 'You're one of a kind and I love that.'

At that moment she felt it. Unique. After all those years of peeking out from under her sister's shadow, of wishing and hoping that there was something special about her, finally here was that feeling. And it was from a totally different source than the one she'd expected. A better source. An infinitely more important one.

'So what happens now?' she asked, looking him dead in the eye.

'Game of chess?' he asked, smiling seductively.

'I can think of something much more fun than that,' she said, raising a suggestive eyebrow.

'Fun sounds good,' he said, and before she had time to react he pulled her tight against his body, locking his arms around her back. 'What the lady wants, the lady gets,' he said, kissing her hard. 'Tell me what you want,' he whispered against her mouth.

'Take me to bed and I'll show you,' she said, kissing him back.

* * * * *

Mills & Boon® Hardback
March 2014

ROMANCE

A Prize Beyond Jewels	Carole Mortimer
A Queen for the Taking?	Kate Hewitt
Pretender to the Throne	Maisey Yates
An Exception to His Rule	Lindsay Armstrong
The Sheikh's Last Seduction	Jennie Lucas
Enthralled by Moretti	Cathy Williams
The Woman Sent to Tame Him	Victoria Parker
What a Sicilian Husband Wants	Michelle Smart
Waking Up Pregnant	Mira Lyn Kelly
Holiday with a Stranger	Christy McKellen
The Returning Hero	Soraya Lane
Road Trip With the Eligible Bachelor	Michelle Douglas
Safe in the Tycoon's Arms	Jennifer Faye
Awakened By His Touch	Nikki Logan
The Plus-One Agreement	Charlotte Phillips
For His Eyes Only	Liz Fielding
Uncovering Her Secrets	Amalie Berlin
Unlocking the Doctor's Heart	Susanne Hampton

MEDICAL

Waves of Temptation	Marion Lennox
Risk of a Lifetime	Caroline Anderson
To Play with Fire	Tina Beckett
The Dangers of Dating Dr Carvalho	Tina Beckett

0214GEN STD HB

Mills & Boon® Large Print

March 2014

ROMANCE

Million Dollar Christmas Proposal	Lucy Monroe
A Dangerous Solace	Lucy Ellis
The Consequences of That Night	Jennie Lucas
Secrets of a Powerful Man	Chantelle Shaw
Never Gamble with a Caffarelli	Melanie Milburne
Visconti's Forgotten Heir	Elizabeth Power
A Touch of Temptation	Tara Pammi
A Little Bit of Holiday Magic	Melissa McClone
A Cadence Creek Christmas	Donna Alward
His Until Midnight	Nikki Logan
The One She Was Warned About	Shoma Narayanan

HISTORICAL

Rumours that Ruined a Lady	Marguerite Kaye
The Major's Guarded Heart	Isabelle Goddard
Highland Heiress	Margaret Moore
Paying the Viking's Price	Michelle Styles
The Highlander's Dangerous Temptation	Terri Brisbin

MEDICAL

The Wife He Never Forgot	Anne Fraser
The Lone Wolf's Craving	Tina Beckett
Sheltered by Her Top-Notch Boss	Joanna Neil
Re-awakening His Shy Nurse	Annie Claydon
A Child to Heal Their Hearts	Dianne Drake
Safe in His Hands	Amy Ruttan

0214 GEN STD LP

Mills & Boon® Hardback
April 2014

ROMANCE

A D'Angelo Like No Other	Carole Mortimer
Seduced by the Sultan	Sharon Kendrick
When Christakos Meets His Match	Abby Green
The Purest of Diamonds?	Susan Stephens
Secrets of a Bollywood Marriage	Susanna Carr
What the Greek's Money Can't Buy	Maya Blake
The Last Prince of Dahaar	Tara Pammi
The Sicilian's Unexpected Duty	Michelle Smart
One Night with Her Ex	Lucy King
The Secret Ingredient	Nina Harrington
Her Soldier Protector	Soraya Lane
Stolen Kiss From a Prince	Teresa Carpenter
Behind the Film Star's Smile	Kate Hardy
The Return of Mrs Jones	Jessica Gilmore
Her Client from Hell	Louisa George
Flirting with the Forbidden	Joss Wood
The Last Temptation of Dr Dalton	Robin Gianna
Resisting Her Rebel Hero	Lucy Ryder

MEDICAL

200 Harley Street: Surgeon in a Tux	Carol Marinelli
200 Harley Street: Girl from the Red Carpet	Scarlet Wilson
Flirting with the Socialite Doc	Melanie Milburne
His Diamond Like No Other	Lucy Clark

0314GEN STD HB

Mills & Boon® Large Print
April 2014

ROMANCE

Defiant in the Desert	Sharon Kendrick
Not Just the Boss's Plaything	Caitlin Crews
Rumours on the Red Carpet	Carole Mortimer
The Change in Di Navarra's Plan	Lynn Raye Harris
The Prince She Never Knew	Kate Hewitt
His Ultimate Prize	Maya Blake
More than a Convenient Marriage?	Dani Collins
Second Chance with Her Soldier	Barbara Hannay
Snowed in with the Billionaire	Caroline Anderson
Christmas at the Castle	Marion Lennox
Beware of the Boss	Leah Ashton

HISTORICAL

Not Just a Wallflower	Carole Mortimer
Courted by the Captain	Anne Herries
Running from Scandal	Amanda McCabe
The Knight's Fugitive Lady	Meriel Fuller
Falling for the Highland Rogue	Ann Lethbridge

MEDICAL

Gold Coast Angels: A Doctor's Redemption	Marion Lennox
Gold Coast Angels: Two Tiny Heartbeats	Fiona McArthur
Christmas Magic in Heatherdale	Abigail Gordon
The Motherhood Mix-Up	Jennifer Taylor
The Secret Between Them	Lucy Clark
Craving Her Rough Diamond Doc	Amalie Berlin

0314 GEN STD LP

Discover more romance at

www.millsandboon.co.uk

- ❤ WIN great prizes in our exclusive competitions
- ❤ BUY new titles before they hit the shops
- ❤ BROWSE new books and REVIEW your favourites
- ❤ SAVE on new books with the Mills & Boon® Bookclub™
- ❤ DISCOVER new authors

PLUS, to chat about your favourite reads, get the latest news and find special offers:

- Find us on facebook.com/millsandboon
- Follow us on twitter.com/millsandboonuk
- ❤ Sign up to our newsletter at millsandboon.co.uk